THE MYSTERY OF RAINBOW GULCH

THE TED WILFORD SERIES

THE MYSTERY OF RAINBOW GULCH

NORVIN PALLAS

WILDSIDE PRESS

CHAPTER 1.

THE NIGHT PLANE

"That must have been Hopalong we just went through," said Ted Wilford, staring with a frown at the road map in his lap.

"How can you tell?" demanded his friend, Nelson Morgan, who was driving. "It isn't marked on the map."

"No, but it's where the roads meet."

"Well, maybe you're right," Nelson admitted, "but I've seen parking lots that were bigger than that. Think we're on the right road, then?"

"We must be. There doesn't seem to be any place to go wrong. We should get there in another fifteen minutes."

Nelson glanced up for a moment from the lightly traveled gravel road. "I thought this was a ranch we were going to, but these look more like farms we're passing. Look at those neatly kept fields."

"I suppose it's half and half. Bob mentioned cows and sheep. Anyway, the important thing is that they have horses to ride. Have you ever been on a horse?"

"No—except on a merry-go-round. How about you?"

"Just a few rides in the park at Stanton when I was a kid."

"Those were ponies," Nelson pointed out.

Ted laughed. "Yes, I guess they were ponies at that. But they looked big enough to me at the time."

"That corn doesn't look too good to me," said Nelson critically. "We saw better on the way out. Think they've got a soil problem here?"

"More likely it's a water problem. This has been a pretty dry summer."

"Anyway, I'm glad you wangled an invitation for me to come along, Ted."

"What do you mean?" Ted objected. "Bob is more your friend than mine. He was on the freshman squad with you."

"Sure, and who was it that went over his term papers and pointed out errors to him? He appreciated that more than anything I did for him. That's how we got the invitations."

"Oh, that." Ted dismissed it with a shrug. "All I did was proofread them, the way I'd correct a story for the *Town Crier*."

"Sh," Nelson cautioned. "No shop talk, remember. This was going to be a vacation, and nothing but. No newspaper stories, no adventures—just relax and enjoy ourselves."

"You're sure you don't want any adventures?" asked Ted.

"Look, if I get up on a horse, that's going to be adventure enough."

But Ted looked thoughtful and Nelson asked, "All right, what's eating you?"

"Oh, nothing, really. You said it was just a vacation, so let's leave it that way."

"You mean you think Bob had something more in mind when he invited us out here?"

"How should I know? I'm only guessing."

"Listen, Ted, you may have a good nose for news, but I think we're all going to be better off if you give it a good rest."

Ted might have retorted, but Nelson was busy examining the names on the rural mailboxes as they passed. Then suddenly the name "Fontaine" appeared, and they were there. Nelson turned up the drive.

A dog was the first to notice their arrival, and came charging down at them, barking loudly, until a voice ordered, "Be quiet, Cougar." At that he stopped barking, but kept up a nervous whine. A moment later the owner of the voice appeared.

It was a little girl about five years old, evidently Bob's younger sister.

"I'll hold him, and you can drive on up," she instructed them, and Nelson, who had stopped the car through fear of hitting the dog if not the child, started up again slowly while the girl kept a grip on Cougar's collar. There was little doubt that he could have pulled away had he chose, but he seemed well trained and showed no such inclination.

Pulling as close to the house as the drive would allow, Nelson drew to a stop, and the boys got out. A woman was coming from the back of the house to greet them, but before she could reach them Bob came dashing out of the front door and ran up to them, pumping their hands.

"Glad you got here. We were just beginning to think that you had had trouble on the road, or got lost, or something like that."

"Oh, no, no trouble," Nelson assured him, "but we weren't exactly speeding, either. This is our first trip this far west, and we wanted to see as much as we could."

"Fellows, this is my mother," Bob introduced her, as she joined them. "Mother, this is Nelson Morgan, who played on the football squad, and this is Ted Wilford, the newspaper reporter—well, part time, anyway."

"How do you do?" She shook hands with each of them in turn. "We're always glad to have visitors, and Bob has been looking forward to your visit with almost suspicious eagerness."

"You're my insurance policy," Bob explained with a laugh.

"Insurance for what?" asked Ted curiously.

"Insurance against work. They can't expect me to put in a full day of work when I've got visitors to entertain, can they?"

"Oh, we don't want you to change your routine on our account," Nelson assured him. "We can mosey around and take care of ourselves."

"We can even help out with the work," Ted put in quickly. "I'd like to know a little more about how a farm is run—if we wouldn't be in the way."

"Sure," Nelson agreed, with some reluctance. "I've even heard that work can be fun—when you don't have to do it."

"There's Tony," Bob remarked. "Come on over here, Tony, and say hello to our visitors."

But the little girl had turned suddenly shy. She came closer, but stood with her hands behind her back. There was no further trouble with Cougar, however. He came right up to them and nosed their hands, sensing that they were accepted. What he might have done had they been intruders, they could not guess—for he was a rather large dog of uncertain breed.

"We met Tony down the drive," Ted remarked with a smile for her.

"Well, I suppose we ought to be getting in," Mrs. Fontaine decided. "Bob can show you to your room, and you'll have a little time to freshen up before supper. Tony, I can use a little help in the kitchen."

She skipped off after her mother, as the boys unloaded the bags from the car and carried them into the house and up to the guest room.

"Don't get dressed up for supper," Bob cautioned them. "Change into something old, because afterward I'll get out the horses."

"Will there be time?" Ted questioned.

"There'll be two hours of daylight left. That'll give you time for all the riding you'll care to do on your first try."

"What's my horse's name?" asked Nelson, as though that would make any difference.

"Ah—Blaze, and I'll put Ted on Meadowlark. My horse is Starlight. Of course she's the best of the lot, in my opinion. I don't want to seem selfish, but you know how it is."

His visitors assured him that they knew exactly how it was, though Nelson seemed suspicious.

"This Blaze—you're sure you're not giving me a rough one, just as a kind of joke?"

"No joke about it at all," Bob assured him solemnly.

At the supper table they were introduced to Mr. Fontaine, who also gave them a cordial welcome. The conversation was lively but Bob seemed to have something on his mind, and was eager for a chance to tell about it.

"Dad, I heard that the Kirsteads lost another ewe last night."

"That so?" Mr. Fontaine did not seem particularly disturbed. "Maybe they ought to check their fences."

"They keep their fences in pretty good shape, Dad. Anyway, you know how sheep are. If one did find a place to squeeze through, the whole flock is likely to follow. And coming after the ones lost last winter—"

"The snow had drifted pretty high against the fences, Bob."

"I don't know, Dad. I've got sort of a queer hunch about it."

There was a twinkle in his father's eyes. "All right, Bob, suppose you-tell us your hunch."

Bob nodded mysteriously toward the hills which bordered the farm on one side. "Funny about those hills. They seem so close, and yet you never really know what's going on up there. It's maybe only once in a blue moon, and only during hunting season at that, that anyone gets up there, deep into them. It wouldn't surprise me if there was a mountain lion up there—maybe even a pair of them!"

His guests were startled, but Mr. Fontaine seemed only amused.

"Seen any tracks—anything to go on?"

"No," Bob admitted, "but I noticed game seemed plentiful earlier in the spring before the dry spell set in, and where the game is good a mountain lion is likely to follow. And then, look how that fits in with the missing sheep. Last winter, when game was hard to get, we and the other farmers lost some sheep. Then while game was plentiful, we weren't bothered, but now with the dry spell another sheep is gone."

Like all sheepmen, Mr. Fontaine had no liking for mountain lions, which had the reputation of killing more than they really needed for food.

"It doesn't sound like a mountain lion, as long as there's only one missing at a time, and that at long intervals. If he found such easy pickings, he'd begin to make a regular diet of them."

"A smart mountain lion wouldn't do it that way," Bob maintained. "He'd take a sheep only when he had to, and keep as far away from the farms as he could the rest of the time. Maybe it's a cagey, older fellow who's had some experience with men already. He'd know that if he made a big enough nuisance of himself, we could rout out every man in the county and make things pretty hot for him."

"I wonder if a mountain lion would be smart enough to figure that out," Nelson speculated.

"You bet he would. Look at some of those stories Jake Pastor tells about the mountain lions that used to prey around here. I know you can only believe about half of what he says, but he's got a piece of tail—"

"You notice he isn't showing the *whole* tail," Mr. Fontaine pointed out.

"Jake Pastor tells some pretty tall stories," Mrs. Fontaine explained to the newcomers. "He claims that he had a ram that learned to get over the fence by leaping up on the back of another sheep. So then Jake built the fence higher, and this ram taught the other sheep to make a pyramid."

"Where do you think this mountain lion is hiding?" Mr. Fontaine questioned his son.

"Up in one of the gulches—Dead Man's maybe, or Gopher, or Rainbow. Say, that's it, Rainbow Gulch. That's the most secluded spot, and there're rocky ledges where he could hole up. Come to think of it, it's the only one with a reliable water supply."

"Well, Rainbow Gulch is as good a place as any, I suppose, but if he's up there, he must be a regular hermit. But I still say that a mountain lion as clever as you're imagining would be more likely to pick off a stray lamb, rather than tackle a full-grown sheep. There'd be less danger of making a stir."

"Why shouldn't he take a sheep instead of a lamb, Dad, if he's big enough to handle it? He might be able to pick it up with hardly any traces, leaving the carcass miles from here. There wouldn't have to be much commotion. He could sneak up downwind, and get off with a sheep before the dogs ever knew what was happening. He'd have to be smart, all right. Last winter he used to come just before a snow storm so he couldn't be tracked."

"That seems to leave us with a mountain lion that's remarkably big, remarkably intelligent, and a weather prophet as well." Mr. Fontaine grinned. "It's a pretty good story, Bob. But if you wanted a day off to take your friends riding, why didn't you just ask for it? I might have said yes, and you could have saved this story until you really needed it."

Bob smiled sheepishly, but did not give up entirely. "But the Kirsteads really did lose a ewe last night, Dad." He and his father exchanged understanding glances, and no more was said.

After supper Bob was eager to get to the horses, but his visitors followed him outside with some reluctance, Nelson protesting that he had just eaten too much.

"Oh, it'll settle before we get really riding," Bob declared. "I'll get Blaze out first."

He led the horse out from the stable, and Nelson looked him over.

"He looks pretty big. How do I know he likes me?"

"Just pet him on the muzzle a little until he gets to know you."

Nelson did, but the horse didn't seem to care very much one way or the other. Having delayed as long as he could, Nelson put a foot up into the stirrup, and swung himself onto the animal's back. If he expected the horse to begin to buck like a bronco, he was agreeably surprised, for Blaze hardly seemed to pay any attention to him at all.

"That's half the battle won," Bob encouraged him. "Now get him to walk around a little."

Nelson did, and seemed amazed that he could persuade the horse to follow his directions. He was soon walking his mount around the farmyard with ever-growing confidence.

"It sure beats waiting for a taxi in the rain," he gloated.

Then it was Ted's turn. Meadowlark had been saddled and brought out by one of the hired hands. Ted swung up into the saddle immediately, and although his horse seemed a little more restive than Nelson's, Ted soon had him under control, and was following in Nelson's path as they circled the yard.

Then Bob left them, for he wanted to saddle Starlight himself. He was soon back, mounted, and Ted and Nelson could see at once that he had not exaggerated about his horse. Starlight was younger, and built along sleeker lines than the other horses. They had an idea that Starlight was the fastest horse on that farm, and quite possibly the fastest in the entire neighborhood. But under the circumstances they preferred their own mounts.

"Let's take a ride up to the ridge," Bob suggested. "We might be able to see one of the transcontinental jets go over."

"Why don't we ride into Hopalong and watch the train come in?" asked Nelson.

His sarcasm was lost on Bob. "Can't do that. There's only one train a day, and they're even talking about taking that one off. All ready? Then let's go."

He set the pace on Starlight, but not a very fast one, though it was much faster than Ted and Nelson felt ready for. Little clouds of dust began to shoot up from the dried-out trail. Bob urged his mare up the long incline leading to the top of the ridge, and his friends did the same. There was a sharp rise just before the summit was reached, but Starlight made it easily, and the others without a great deal of trouble. Bob drew up and dismounted with an easy motion which the other two tried to copy.

They were looking directly into the western sky where the red sun was setting with less display than it frequently made, for it was a cloudless evening.

"We should see it long before we hear it," Bob observed, turning about so that he was looking into the vacant eastern sky. "But sometimes they stray too far to the north or south to see them here."

The roar of a plane came upon them suddenly from a different direction than they had expected. It was in fact coming in from the southeast; and it wasn't the transcontinental plane, but a single-engine cabin model. It passed over them, and then seemed to circle around some point up ahead.

"That's Sandy kill," Bob explained. "I wonder what the pilot wants over there?"

The noise of the engine cut off suddenly, but whether it had passed out of hearing or the pilot was gliding they could not tell. The plane was settling down, lower and lower. There seemed a chance that he might ram into the hill unless he was very careful about what he was doing. He was so low now that his next wide bank took him out of sight beyond Sandy Hill.

They waited expectantly for the plane to reappear. Then something inside them seemed to freeze as the seconds continued to tick away. Nelson put their common fear into words.

"Hey! I'll bet that plane crashed!"

CHAPTER 2.

MISSION OF MERCY

For a few moments the boys stood immobilized. Then reason took command, and the visitors looked to Bob for leadership. This was an emergency, and in all likelihood they were the only ones who had seen the crash, the only ones who could do anything about it.

"Any chance he could have landed safely?" asked Ted.

Bob shook his head. "Not a real landing. A crash landing, maybe, if he could find a little clear space in the trees. And that wouldn't be easy to find on Sandy Hill. It's pretty well wooded over, except for the very top."

"What about beyond Sandy Hill?" Nelson inquired.

"Nothing much there that would be useful to him—no farms, just rolling hills, rocks, and forest. There is a road winding through the hills, and he may have been trying to reach it. That would be just about his only chance."

"What about a parachute? He might have had a chance to jump at the last instant," Ted pointed out.

"He was awfully low. That would give him very little margin to play with, unless he knew he might crash and was all ready to act. Those small planes don't have ejector seats, or anything like that."

"I wonder if his engine really did conk out?" Nelson speculated. "If it did, he may have been ready for the crash. But if he was just flying too low and suddenly couldn't pull up, he wouldn't have had much chance to escape. Shouldn't we be doing something? I can just imagine him dangling from a tree, caught by his parachute,"

"Well, let's be sure we know what we're doing before we try," said Bob, reasonably. "The location of the plane is the most important thing. I think I've got a pretty good line on it from here. That plane has to be on the northwest slope of Sandy Hill, or a reasonably short distance beyond it. I don't see any sign of smoke, do you?"

The others agreed with him that they didn't. If there was no fire, that was an encouraging sign, and offered greater hope for the safety of the pilot.

"Are we going there on horseback?" Nelson wanted to know.

"Whoa, there, Nel. There's no chance of getting there on horses. It's farther than it looks, and there are several deep gulches in the way. We couldn't make it before midnight, if we got through at all. The best bet is to drive around by road, and take the rest of it on shank's mare. And before we do that, we ought to notify the authorities. They might have better facilities for a search than we do."

The boys swung into their saddles, and raced back toward the farm, Bob in the lead and the others following as fast as they dared. When Ted and Nelson reached the house, Bob was already inside. They dismounted, and a farm hand took charge of their horses. Hurrying inside, they found that Bob had already made some hasty explanations to his parents, and after cranking up their party-line phone, asked the operator to reach the Civil Aeronautics Patrol. The call went through in due course, and Bob held the receiver a little way from his ear so that his friends could hear, too.

"My name is Bob Fontaine," he announced. "I want to report the possible crash of a plane in the Sandy Hill region."

"A crash! Was it a large transport?" asked the man with alarm.

"No, this appeared to be a one-engine private plane."

"Are you sure it went down?"

Bob looked at his friends. Of course they hadn't actually seen the plane hit the ground, though it seemed hardly likely the plane could have escaped. On the other hand, he had admitted to them the bare possibility that the pilot had managed to reach the road and landed safely.

"Well, no, it disappeared beyond Sandy Hill, and when it failed to reappear, we decided it must have crashed. It would have been quite some distance from the nearest road, and there isn't much in the way of clearings up there. Anyway, I thought it best to make a report on it."

"Yes, you did the right thing. However, I don't have any report on flights in that area tonight. Did you see where the plane came from?"

"From the southeast, I think, and then it circled over Sandy Hill."

"Did it show any signs of distress?"

"We couldn't tell for sure. It was too far away."

"No sign of fire or explosion?"

"Not that we saw."

"Well, I'll check into this right away. If there was a crash, I'll call you back. We may need your help in locating it. Where can I reach you?"

"Through the Valley Junction exchange, ring two, pause, ring two."

"Oh, one of those things." The man sounded as though he would have been amused at another time. "Well, you'll very likely be hearing from me soon. Good-bye," and he rang off.

The boys returned to the living room, where the rest of the family were sitting. Tony had been in bed, but not asleep, and she was allowed to curl up in the big easy chair. If there was something exciting going on, she didn't want to be left out.

"I wonder if it could have been one of the forest rangers' planes," Mr. Fontaine asked.

"I don't think so, Dad. It didn't look like one of their models."

"Then I can't think who else it could be. None of the farmers around here has an airplane. It was probably a stranger—which doesn't make it any better, of course."

"Whoever he is, I hope he wasn't hurt," said Mrs. Fontaine sympathetically.

"Did the man in the airplane get killed?" asked Tony.

"We hope not," said Bob quietly. "That's what we're going to try to find out."

"I hope he didn't either," Tony agreed quickly.

"Are you boys still sure that the plane crashed?" asked Mr. Fontaine. "It seems to me that there's a big flaw in your story. You've more or less assumed that his engine had stopped. What if he started up again after he was out of your hearing? He might have disappeared behind the hill, hedgehopping on a line directly away from you, so that he never came back into view again."

"Golly, Dad, why would he do something like that?"

"I can't answer that, Bob, any more than I can answer what he was doing circling over Sandy Hill at that time of the evening."

"Gosh, Dad, maybe you're right. I hope so, but I'm going to be a laughingstock, if I raised all this fuss about a plane that didn't crash."

"I think you boys handled everything just right," his mother interposed.

"What makes airplanes crash?" Tony wanted to know. "Does the air sometimes get tired of holding the airplane up there?"

"Well, no," said Bob, "I don't think that ever happens. Sometimes there's a storm and the wind is too strong for the plane. Or sometimes a part on the airplane breaks. Or sometimes the pilot does something wrong. But most of the time it's perfectly safe. You'll see if you go for a ride sometime."

The telephone jangled then—two short, pause, two short—and Bob left the room to answer. They heard him say, "Bob Fontaine speaking," then a little later said with a note of urgency, "Listen, everybody, please hang up. This is long distance, and I can hardly hear. I'll call you back later to tell you what it's about." Apparently his neighbors on the line complied, for the conversation continued.

"Maybe this business of listening in on the line doesn't sound right to you," Mr. Fontaine explained to the visitors, "but we find it a good kind of insurance. Out in a lonely region like this, we have to depend on each other a good deal, and if one of our neighbors is in trouble we want to know about it fast."

"And it's a kind of newspaper, too, Ted," said Mrs. Fontaine with a smile. "It's probably not as good as the *Town Crier*, but it's the best we have."

"How many parties are on your line?" asked Ted.

"Ten, on our line. But if something important enough turns up, someone will call a neighbor on a different circuit, and the whole thing gets around pretty fast. It's kind of reassuring to know it."

"That was Mr. MacCafferty again," Bob reported when he came back. "It's dark already, and he doesn't think they can do much by air, but he wants to make an attempt to reach the wreck on foot, just in case the pilot needs help."

"Then he really does think there was a crash, Bob?" his father inquired.

"Yes, he does, Dad. There was a private flight scheduled between Starburg and Mayorstown, and the plane is overdue. Of course a plane on that route has no business being anywhere near Sandy Hill, but he said something about the pilot's being a student who may have lost his way. Anyway, he's coming over here with a rescue truck, and wants me to go with him. I told him about Ted and Nelson, and they're welcome, too, if they want to come."

"Just try to keep us out," said Nelson.

While his mother called back the neighbors as he had promised, Bob took his visitors out to the stables to attend to the horses. Even though there were hired hands available, he liked to do everything for Starlight himself. Ted and Nelson were glad to give a hand, too, after he had explained to them what there was to do. They wanted to have something to do because they could not quite shake off the shock of the tragedy they had witnessed, or thought they had witnessed, worries which might soon be confirmed if they were able to find the plane on Sandy Hill.

Within an hour Mr. MacCafferty arrived, and hearing the car and seeing the gleam of headlights turning up the drive, the boys left the stable. Although he was driving a rescue truck, Mr. MacCafferty was alone.

"I felt we'd have enough with you boys," he pointed out, "and I didn't want to waste time rounding up any more workers. We did have the forest rangers send a flight out over Sandy Hill, and I got the report on my radio on the way out. They weren't able to pick up anything."

Introductions were performed, and then he suggested stopping in the house for a few words with Mr. and Mrs. Fontaine before the group set out. In the living room, further introductions were made. Then Mr. MacCafferty said:

"My truck is supplied with lanterns, first-aid equipment, and almost everything else we can expect to need. I've studied a map, but it doesn't tell too much about the terrain. What kind of going will it be?"

"It's pretty rough country," said Bob slowly, "especially after dark. But I think we can make it."

"According to the map, the road comes within three miles or so of Sandy Hill. Is that about how you'd figure it?"

"I think we can do better than that. There was some lumbering going on there about a year ago, and I believe there are probably some lumber roads that your map doesn't show. They should bring us even closer."

"Good, that may help."

"You said it was a student pilot at the controls?" asked Mr. Fontaine.

"When I said student, I meant a novice pilot. As a matter of fact he is middle-aged, which in my books makes his offenses all the worse."

"Offenses?" Ted questioned.

"Well, he may have been stunting, or something like that, and I don't think his plane was properly lighted and equipped for night flying. Furthermore, there is something peculiar about this whole flight. We know what time he left Starburg, and it just wasn't possible that he would have enough gasoline left to be buzzing Sandy Hill at twilight. Let's be generous and say he lost his way, or that his transmitting equipment broke down and he was unable to notify the airport of a change in flight plans, or even that an emergency forced him down at some place remote from a telephone.

"Now what? This spot must have had some gasoline, must have had facilities for him to repair whatever it was that went wrong. Then what business did he have taking off just before twilight, if he was as badly oriented as the evidence would show? Even if he were seriously confused as to where he was, what did he hope to accomplish by circling over Sandy Hill? All this makes a strange type of emergency. Such a series of unusual happenings seems to stretch the long arm of coincidence too far." He concluded grimly, "If Mr. Leonard is still alive, he'd better come up with some pretty good explanations."

"Then you know the name of the pilot?" asked Mr. Fontaine.

"Yes, it's Jeff Leonard. Have any of you ever heard of him?" The Fontaines all shook their heads. "He is a strange sort of person, too. He is constantly bringing himself to the attention of the police, without actually committing any sort of crime that he can be convicted of. He seems to be living better than his known source of income permits, which is always a suspicious circumstance. He is suspected of getting mixed up with unscrupulous persons. This isn't to disparage him, but when a person endangers the lives of others, when there is property loss involved and a great many people are put to the worry and expense of helping him, then we are within our rights in asking some pretty searching questions."

"What do you think happened?" Ted inquired.

"At this stage it can only be a theory, but my opinion is that he was never lost at all, that he knew exactly where he was and what he was doing. I think he made an unauthorized stop somewhere, for a purpose which we do not know, and about which he did not care to be questioned. I've no doubt that if he had not crashed, he would have called in soon after his flight over Sandy Hill and had some story all ready about an emergency stop which we probably would have accepted in the absence of any evidence to the contrary. Unfortunately for him we know about his flight over Sandy Hill, and that would probably have knocked the props out from under whatever story he had planned. Any explanations he has to make now would probably have to bear at least some resemblance to the truth. My job is going to be a good deal easier if he is still alive and can give me a few clues about what he was up to. Otherwise, I may have to do a lot of unprofitable guessing."

"Was there a search out for this plane before I called?" asked Bob.

"There was an alert between Starburg and Mayorstown. Any planes in that area were asked to keep a watch out for the overdue plane. In the case of large transports we inaugurate a search whenever we know that the plane has run out of fuel. Private flights are less controlled than that, and we don't start a search until we have something more to go on. We just don't have the facilities to do more."

"Then there's no question about the identity of this plane we saw?" asked Ted.

"I shouldn't think so," said Mr. MacCafferty with a frown. "Your description, such as it is, corresponds with the missing plane, and if it isn't Leonard's plane, I have no idea whose it could be. We shall probably know soon."

Unless the plane had hedgehopped away to safety, Ted thought, and saw by a glance from Bob that he was thinking the same thing. In that case there would be no proof whether it was Leonard's plane or not.

CHAPTER 3.

THE SEARCH AT SANDY HILL

Cougar had decided to be friendly, and gave Mr. Mac-Cafferty no more than a sniff as the group left the house and piled into the truck. Though Mr. MacCafferty paused to pat him on the head, he was too preoccupied to give the dog any further attention.

"Should we turn left or right to get on the main road?" he asked as they came to the end of the drive.

"Left," replied Bob, "and we'll join the main road about two miles down."

He was sitting next to Mr. MacCafferty, and at his suggestion reached for a map of the district, which he studied with the aid of a pencil flashlight.

"It would certainly help me, boys, if you could tell just about where you think that plane crashed."

Ted and Nelson were riding behind them, and looked over his shoulder as Bob tried to figure out exactly where they had been standing at the moment the plane disappeared, and where they had last seen it.

"I think it was just about here that it went out of sight," he decided finally, and consulted the others. "Don't you think so?"

"You've lost me already," said Nelson firmly, and Ted, too, had to admit that he was too uncertain of the area to supply any accurate guess.

"How much farther do you think it might have gone before it crashed?"

"It was losing altitude rapidly. I don't think it would have flown much farther. Maybe right about in here."

Bob drew a little circle on the map, representing his best judgment, though his friends were aware of his doubts. Maybe the plane didn't crash, and this was a wild-goose chase. With so many queer things about this flight, who could say that there wasn't one more?

"Are the forest rangers doing anything more, or are we searching alone?" asked Ted.

"They're on stand-by alert, and I may call on them later, depending on what we find or fail to find. If you boys are right, we may be able to walk right up to the wreck. If we don't spot it, I'll notify the rangers and see what they want to do. Even if we do find it, we may run into difficulties and need their help on the ground. Anyway it's good to know they're within reach if we should need them."

The truck was on the main highway now, and on each side of them the black woods flitted by. Their emergency lights flashed warningly, but there was no need to use the siren, so lightly traveled was the road. Mr. MacCafferty referred to the map Bob had folded on his lap.

"Now where is this lumber road you were speaking of? I don't care much for traveling cross-country in the dark, and if you can save us part of the distance, so much the better."

Bob considered. "I think it starts somewhere right along here. I've never been on it myself, but someone told me it takes a big half circle through the woods before hitting the main road again several miles farther out."

"Well, then, if we take this road and follow it out for say a mile, we'll be as close to the wreck as we can get, isn't that right?"

"Yes, sir, I think so—but it makes me feel funny to think that you're depending so much on what I tell you. I may be way off base."

"We'll meet that difficulty when we come to it. I have an idea that you people are going to prove more reliable than most witnesses. Every time a plane flies over a little low, especially one of the big transports, we get calls that it crashed, or was in distress. Some of the reports would be laughable if they weren't so serious, because naturally we have to investigate them all."

This did not serve to reassure Bob much. He had tried to be as careful as he could, but if it turned out there hadn't been a crash, he was going to feel mighty embarrassed—not only because of Mr. MacCafferty but because the story was undoubtedly all over the county by now.

Mr. MacCafferty slowed down and kept his spotlight shining on the line of trees opposite, so as not to miss the lumber road. He found it presently and turned down, and from there on their ride became much slower and bumpier. When the truck stopped, they all piled out.

Ted and Nelson were each to carry one of the powerful lanterns, while Bob took the first-aid kit and other supplies, and Mr. MacCafferty the map and compass, from which he took a careful bearing. "It won't help to have us lost, too," he explained. Bob and Mr. MacCafferty also carried hand flashlights, for the other lights were too strong and glaring to pick out their immediate path.

The ground led away from the road on an easy but steady rise, and Mr. MacCafferty inquired whether they were already on Sandy Hill.

"No," Bob replied, "we'll have to cross at least one or two gullies before we get to the hill. But we may be able to sweep the hillside with the searchlights from the top of the first ridge."

They discovered a path which seemed to lead in the direction they wanted to go, and Bob found himself taking the lead, the others confident that he was at least slightly more familiar with the lay of the land than they were. So far, and for a considerable distance up on Sandy Hill, the ground was heavily wooded, although many bleak stumps spoke of logging operations. And suddenly Ted recalled the speculations about a mountain lion somewhere in the woods, then quickly dismissed them. A mountain lion, even if there was one, would be unlikely to attack four of them; the blinding beam of the flashlight should be enough to scare him off. But Ted couldn't help remembering that they were unarmed, unless Mr. Mac-Cafferty had a revolver.

At the top of the incline was a little clearing, and Bob asked, "Shall we set up the lights and see what we can pick up?"

"Might be a good idea," Mr. MacCafferty agreed. He had the map out again and indicated with the point of a pencil: "As far as I can tell, we're right about here." The lead was almost touching the small circle Bob had drawn.

The two lantern searchlights were set up and adjusted, and they began to sweep the hillside opposite. A careful search revealed nothing unusual, and they turned toward Sandy Hill itself, lying above and beyond, its slopes covered except for the barren top. Twice they covered every foot of ground that their beams could touch, but no sign of wreckage was disclosed. Surely they must have covered most of the territory which lay within the circle Bob had drawn. If there was a wreck, it seemed that Bob may have been mistaken about where it would be found.

"But not necessarily," said Mr. MacCafferty briefly. "It's possible for a plane to disappear completely within the trees, or it may be on the lowest part of Sandy Hill." Their lights could not reach there because of the intervening hill. Unless they found the plane there, they all knew they were probably in for a long search.

In silence the searchlights were packed up again, and the party trudged on. Mr. MacCafferty obviously no longer thought they were to have an easy time of it.

A fairly deep gully lay in front of them, and loaded down as they were, they anticipated some difficulty. Fortunately the slopes were not too steep, and they found a comparatively easy path down. Bob, who was leading the way, took a short tumble on a slippery clay patch, and the others, warned by his example, were able to avoid a similar mishap. The rivulet at the bottom of the gully was running unexpectedly full. They could see no easy dry crossing, so in they waded. Then they scrambled up the grassy incline on the other side.

At the top of the hill they discovered they would have to go another hundred yards before they reached the summit of another slight ridge. Here the searchlights were set up again.

The lower slope of Sandy Hill was now within range of their lamps, and they scanned it carefully several times without results. Gradually they raised their beams, covering some of the same territory they had explored from the previous ridge, without much hope. It was beginning to look as though the wreck was not on Sandy Hill.

Then Mr. MacCafferty began to sweep the beam widely, almost hopelessly, touching beyond the foot of Sandy Hill. At that distance he had little expectation of discovering anything, and was about to give up when suddenly Nelson exclaimed:

"Wait, sir, I think I saw something!"

"Where?"

"Right there, where your beam just missed."

Bob and Mr. MacCafferty brought the two lights to focus upon the spot. There they could make out the outline of a spruce tree, and some dark, ominous object seemed to be caught in the top limbs.

"That's it," said Mr. MacCafferty dully. "If I've been thinking anything I shouldn't in the last few minutes, boys, I want to apologize to you, but nine-tenths of the calls we get are duds."

"Think there's any chance the pilot got out alive, Mr. MacCafferty?" asked Ted.

"If that's really the wing of the plane," he answered slowly, "I would say that his chances of getting through the crash without serious injury would be pretty small. But escape by parachute is something else again."

"We didn't see any parachute," Nelson put in.

"Anyway, we'd better get over there as quickly as we can."

On Mr. MacCafferty's orders, one of the searchlights was left standing with its beam focused on the spruce tree. "Sometimes those things are visible only from a certain angle, and we may lose sight of the tree later," he explained. The other light was taken down again, and the party began its grim trek toward the scene of the crash.

With the beam to guide them, they had little trouble covering the rest of the distance to the scene. Approaching, they saw that the object in the tree was undoubtedly the wing of the plane, sheared off by heavy branches. The actual wreck lay fifty yards farther on, in the midst of a small clearing. A few feet had made the difference between safety and disaster, for if the pilot had been able to clear the tall spruce, he might have been able to make a successful crash landing.

Flares were set up at the edge of the clearing, illuminating the whole circle. In addition to the missing wing, the motor was also gone, as well as part of the tail. The landing gear had been crushed, along with part of the cabin, but the plane was not as completely demolished as they had expected.

"Now to see what goes," said Mr. MacCafferty. He seemed to brace himself, then approached the plane, using his pocket flashlight to look inside. He stared steadily for a moment, then turned away. "He's still at the controls," he announced. "He never had a chance to use his chute."

He had expected difficulty in forcing the door, but it opened easily. He went inside, while the boys stood some distance away, unwilling to approach any closer to the wreck.

After long minutes he reappeared. "I'm sorry, but there's nothing anyone can do. He must have been killed instantly. If it's any consolation, that'll save him from trying to explain to me where he stopped previously, and why." Mr. MacCafferty was trying to speak lightly, but they knew he was deeply affected.

Now that the plane had been found, the boys' excitement vanished. Somewhere in the back of their minds had been the hope of bringing about a rescue. It was too late for that now.

"I don't think there's much you can do here right now, boys," said Mr. MacCafferty. "I want to make a preliminary inspection before anything is touched. Wait, Bob, there *is* something you can do for me. Go back to the car and bring a litter. I'd like to get the body out of here tonight, if we can."

"Right!"

"You won't have any trouble finding the car, will you? And I don't suppose there's any danger from wild animals around here."

"I don't think so," said Bob, crossing his fingers but in a manner that only his friends could see. "I'll go back the same way we came. There may be a shorter way, but there's no use looking for trouble."

"There's no doubt about the identity of the plane, is there?" asked Ted, after Bob had departed.

"No, the pilot had identification papers on him, so apparently this really is Jeff Leonard. The numbers on the plane check, too, so this is obviously the missing Starburg-Mayors-town plane. Funny, there seems to be enough fuel left in the tanks, so that couldn't have been the cause of the wreck. It's a miracle it didn't catch on fire, although I guess it wouldn't have made any difference to the pilot even if it did. If you boys would scout around a little and try to locate parts of the plane, it may help me reconstruct the accident."

Thankful for any excuse to get away from the plane, Ted and Nelson started off. The engine lay about midway between the spruce tree and the rest of the wreck. It appeared that the wing must have caught in the spruce tree and ripped off, whereupon the plane nose-dived into the ground. There the engine had fallen off, but the rest of the plane bounced and skidded between the trees to its present position in the clearing. Other pieces of wreckage were scattered about at random, and they picked these out by the light of the flashlight Nelson was carrying. It was surprising how far some of the parts had been thrown. A piece of the tail lay many rods away, partway up the slope of Sandy Hill itself.

"Ted, this isn't a newspaper story, is it?" Nelson asked.

"No, I guess not," said Ted reluctantly. "They don't have a local paper here. They get a city paper which comes a day late. I suppose that paper might give it a small notice written from the police reports, but I doubt that any of the other papers or a wire service would pick it up."

But still, Ted could not help noticing all the small details he could, just as though he were going to write a newspaper story on it. As the CAP man had said, any information they picked up might be useful in his report.

They found the fatal spruce tree. The searchlight had either burned out or else Bob had turned it off on his way back to the car, and the flares around the cabin of the plane did not quite reach there. But they turned their flashlight upward to study the fragment closely. It seemed to have nothing more to tell, and Ted began to look around. A little path led off through the woods, and almost idly he began to follow it.

"What are we doing?" asked Nelson, following Ted's lead nevertheless.

"There's a little spring up ahead there."

"So what?"

"It looks like it would moisten the ground. I wonder what a path like this is used for, and who follows it. There might be some footprints to give us a lead. I don't think Mr. Mac-Cafferty would like looters going over the plane, before he has a chance to check it out in daylight."

"You're crazy, Ted. A person wouldn't have to be much of an acrobat to jump over the wet parts."

But when he came up to Ted, and they turned the flashlight upon the mud, the footprints were there. Ted's newspaper instincts had proved sound.

"Of course I didn't *know* they were here," Ted explained, as Nelson shook his head in wonder. "I just thought it would be a good place to look."

The footprints led away from the scene of the wreck, but just when they had been made was uncertain.

"They might have been made hours before the wreck, Ted—maybe even a day or two ago."

"No, I don't think so. That flow of water seems pretty steady, and though it's making the mud in which footprints would easily show, it also gradually washes them out after they *are* made. I don't think those prints are many hours old."

"But I don't see why anybody would step through this mud, Ted, when he could easily avoid it."

"What if he didn't have a light?"

"Well, yes, that's true enough, I suppose, but he'd have to have the eyes of a cat to get through here at all after dark. Maybe when he came *to* the plane it was still light enough and he could see his way, but when he went back it was dark, and he stumbled through the mud. I wonder where this path goes?"

"Partway up and around Sandy Hill, I suppose, and then winds through the rest of the hills. It might be an old hunters' trail. Bob said there weren't any farms out this way. What are you doing, Nel?"

Nelson was busy making his own footprints, close beside the ones that they had found. "Just checking. My prints seem to be about the same size, and my stride is about the same. They say you can estimate a man's height from his stride."

"I know, but—" Ted was studying the prints with narrow eyes. "You notice anything strange about those prints?"

"You mean the shape? It is kind of an unusual shape for a shoe or boot, but I suppose lots of men wear something like that."

"No, I wasn't referring to the shape. Look here, Nel. You notice how deep these other prints are?"

"Holy mackerel!" Nelson whistled. "Those prints seem to be almost twice as deep as mine."

"You're right. This man may wear about the same size shoe as you do, and he may be about the same height, but it looks to me as though he's about twice as heavy. He must weigh over three hundred pounds!"

"Wow! That's a mountain of a man. You may have something there, Ted. Maybe this is going to turn out to be a newspaper story, after all."

By the time they returned to the plane, Bob was also back, and they told him and Mr. MacCafferty about the footprints. Although

Bob was interested, Mr. MacCafferty seemed to have more pressing problems on his mind. Possibly, Ted thought, he didn't want to commit himself on a matter about which there was considerable doubt. The government man had an easy manner, but he wasn't telling everything he knew.

The most unpleasant part of their job lay ahead, that of removing the body from the wreck. However, they all got busy and the body, covered with a canvas, was soon outside on the litter.

"Will these flares last till morning?" asked Bob.

"And then some," Mr. MacCafferty responded. "Chances are I'll be back before they're burned out."

"Then you're returning in the morning?"

"Oh, yes, and maybe half a dozen more times before Fm through. I'll want an expert to go over the plane to try to determine the cause of the crash. Then there'll be insurance inspections, and the present owner may want to look over the wreck to see if there's anything worth salvaging."

"There won't be much," Nelson said and the others silently agreed with him.

Then they picked up the litter and headed for the truck. The return journey began as soon as Mr. MacCafferty had called the rangers to cancel the alert.

"I'd like to thank you boys for everything you've done," he said as they neared the farm. "But there's one more favor I want to ask. Do you think you could write up a report on the accident? Just tell in simple words what you saw from the ridge and what we found at the wreck."

"Is this a joint effort, or should we each write separately?" Ted inquired.

"Well—one report will be enough, I suppose, but if you have differences of opinion, get them all in. I don't want the most positive member convincing all the others. I'm sure that Ted knows, as a newspaperman, that the most positive persons are often the worst witnesses."

"Where shall we send the report?" asked Bob.

"You can send it to—on second thought, don't send it to me. I'll stop by for it in a few days."

"Do you want us to mention the footprints?" Nelson demanded.

Mr. MacCafferty hesitated. "Yes, you'd better mention the footprints," he decided. "Whether they have anything to do with the wreck remains to be determined."

As the car approached the farm, Bob suggested, "Just leave us off at the drive. There's no use turning in."

The car stopped, and Mr. MacCafferty shook hands with each of them, then drove off. Cougar hadn't barked, but on the driveway his cold nose suddenly touched Ted's hand, startling him. Though everyone had gone to bed, the door was open and a light was on.

"Let's have something to eat," was Bob's suggestion, and the others agreed he had a good idea there.

CHAPTER 4.

A HITCH

Ted spent a restless night, and when he heard the family stirring, got up to join them at the breakfast table. With Nelson and Bob still sleeping soundly, Ted described their search for the plane and what they had found. The Fontaines listened attentively, and asked a few questions, but it was clear that they wanted to make as light of it as they could while Tony was there.

"I don't think there's anyone around here weighing three hundred pounds," was Mr. Fontaine's comment on the footprints. "Those prints could be deceptive, and might lead you astray."

"Will Bob get up in time for us to go?" asked Tony.

"Go where, Tony?" Mrs. Fontaine inquired.

"For our airplane ride."

"Why, Tony, I'm sure he didn't mean today. He said sometime."

Tony looked disappointed. "Will we go tomorrow, then?"

"No, Tony," her mother explained gently. "I'm afraid it may be a long time before you go. There aren't any private planes around here, so you'd have to go in a commercial plane, and those cost a lot of money."

Tony had a rubber ball, and wanted Ted to play with her for a little while. He consented, and she chatted away as they bounced the ball back and forth.

"Do you know what my last name is? It's going to be Fontaine pretty soon."

"Is it?" said Ted unthinkingly, and then he suddenly realized that Tony was revealing family secrets that perhaps the Fontaines would rather she didn't. "Say, why don't we find Cougar and see if we can teach him to fetch the ball."

Then Ted noticed Mr. Fontaine standing close by. He realized that he had probably overheard this little conversation with Tony. She was soon busy with the dog, and Ted walked over to his host.

"I hope you don't think I was prying into matters that don't concern me, Mr. Fontaine," he apologized.

"Of course not, Ted. As a matter of fact, I was looking forward to talking to you privately about this matter. I was pleased when Bob told me something about your newspaper experience, for I felt you might be able to give me some advice."

"You mustn't make too much of my newspaper connections, Mr. Fontaine. I've just been lucky that I could work with a wonderful editor named Mr. Dobson."

"I know, Ted," said Mr. Fontaine with a smile. "Bob has told me that you praise him to the skies every chance you get. But I do need a little help on newspaper procedures, and before I go into that I'll have to tell you a little more about Tony.

"You realize now that she isn't our daughter, but that we are trying to adopt her. The truth is that we have no idea at all who she really is, and that she almost literally dropped in on us out of nowhere. She came to us one morning just after daybreak. Cougar put up a terrific barking and wouldn't be quieted, and when I went out to see what was wrong, there she was, a bewildered little girl of about three. She was crying, but didn't appear to be in any way injured or neglected. Other than the clothes she was wearing, she brought nothing with her. She was too little to explain anything to us, and when we asked her name, she said something that sounded like Tony, so that is the name we have used ever since. I found some tire tracks in the road, and there were some reports of a strange black sedan in the neighborhood, but neither clue proved of any use to us. She must have been deliberately left by people in a car, and once they were sure that an alarm had been raised, they drove off."

"These people perhaps knew that a little girl would be welcome here, and would be well provided for?"

"Possibly, Ted," said Mr. Fontaine, frowning. "I'd like to believe it was so. But we certainly didn't know her parents, or the little girl either, so how could they know very much about us? It seems more likely that they just picked us at random, and abandoned her."

"You don't know that the people who abandoned her were her parents?"

"They must have been, Ted, or at least people that Tony had come to regard as her parents. She cried for days, calling for her mother and father, but gradually she has come to look upon us as her parents. She knows that she's not our real daughter, and that we are trying to adopt her. But we never talk about the past to her, nor can we tell how much she remembers."

"She seems to be a happy, healthy child," Ted observed.

"I hope so, Ted. We've tried to do our best, but it's one of those things you can never be quite sure about."

"What attempts were made to find her parents?"

"Well, our police department did its best, of course. I think we can rule out any possibility of kidnapping, for the alarm would certainly have reached the department. The people who abandoned her must have been her real parents, or people who had legal custody of her, and they must have known that their tracks were so well covered they couldn't be found unless they were caught while they were leaving her.

"Anyway, the police failed to discover anything. I suppose Tony's description was flashed to other police departments all over the country, but the chances are they did nothing except to try to match her description against their own missing persons reports. They have enough to do about problems closer to home. Nothing ever came of it."

"The newspapers?" Ted questioned, knowing that this was the matter Mr. Fontaine wanted to consult him about.

"Our city paper carried an account of it. What happened beyond that I don't know. Perhaps you would have a better idea about it than I would."

"Well, once it was in print the story would certainly have been available to any other papers that wanted it. I imagine it went out over the wire, but how many papers picked up the story is a question. Was there a picture?"

"Yes, there was in the local paper."

"I hate to admit it, but a particularly appealing picture might be the decisive thing with many city editors. Many of them would simply run it on the picture page with a short paragraph underneath;

otherwise they might not touch it at all. Did you get much of a response?"

"Nothing came to me directly. A few letters may have gone to the police, but nothing of value."

"Then the chances are that your story wasn't circulated very far, or there would probably have been a flood of inquiries and tips."

Mr. Fontaine said after a moment of thought, "Well, that's in the past. My immediate problem is adopting her. For myself, I don't really care to know much about Tony's parents, who were probably incompetents anyway. I'm willing to take her exactly as she is. But I have to consider whether I am being quite fair with her.

"Emotionally speaking, it may some day become very important for her to know more about her parents, especially if she does retain some memories of them about which she has been unable to speak so far. Then there is the financial possibility of an inheritance of some sort, to which she would no longer be entitled if she were adopted. And there is always the possibility of her parents turning up once more and making trouble in some way.

"But my real problem is the fear that something may happen to interfere with the adoption," Mr. Fontaine said with a frown.

"Do you have any reason to expect difficulties?" Ted questioned.

"All I can say for sure is that things are moving along much more slowly than I should like. I know there has to be an investigation of the adopting parents, but that's a mere formality in a small community where everyone knows everyone else. I was hoping to get this thing straightened out before September when I planned to enter Tony in school, but it looks now as though that may not happen. Last night I received a telephone call from Mr. Kerch, our county clerk. If it had been good news I think he would have told me over the phone, but instead he said he was coming out to see me this morning. I'm very much afraid that some sort of hitch or delay has occurred, or even that we may lose Tony altogether. I would only be willing to give her up to her real parents, if they could show that they were not responsible for what happened and could provide properly for her— but not to anyone else."

"I can see where things would be much easier for you if you had the consent of her parents to her adoption, or even if you knew something more about her background," said Ted thoughtfully.

"Yes, and that leads me to wonder if I have done everything I possibly could to trace her parents. The police have given up but maybe I should hire a private investigator. However, the expense would probably be more than I could handle and the results very uncertain. That leaves the newspapers. Your brother works on a big paper, doesn't he?"

"Yes, but that's a thousand miles away in a city which so far as we know has no connection at all with Tony. Still, he might be able to work up a story, and other papers might pick it up, if you're sure that's what you want."

"No, it isn't what I want at all, Ted. I don't believe in making a public display of one's private troubles, and I would much prefer to forget the whole thing. But if it came down to the question of keeping Tony or losing her, then I would be willing to do anything. I'll talk this over with you again, Ted."

A car was pulling into the drive, and Mr. Fontaine identified the driver as Mr. Kerch. The clerk shook hands with Mr. Fontaine, and was introduced to Ted, then looked somewhat questioningly at the boy.

"Don't go away, Ted," Mr. Fontaine urged him. "I've just been discussing the case with him, as he has newspaper connections which I felt might possibly be useful. Is there any news? The court hasn't turned down our petition, has it?"

"No, not turned it down exactly. Let's just say that it's been postponed. I suppose you'll get Tony in the end, but it may mean a dirty court battle, and I know that's something you have no liking for."

"You still haven't told me who it is that's forcing this battle on us, Blake," Mr. Fontaine pointed out. "It's difficult to fight for Tony if I don't know whom I'm fighting against."

"I don't think I'm supposed to say just yet, but it'll be a matter of public record eventually. Anyway, the demurrer objecting to the adoption was filed by Mrs. Manners."

"Mrs. Manners!" Mr. Fontaine almost shouted.

"That's right." Mr. Kerch seemed anxious to leave, and got back into the car. "I thought I'd better let you know how things stood. But you can count on it, Rob, that I will do everything I can for you."

He drove off, and Mr. Fontaine meditated in silence for a few moments.

"Mrs. Manners—I just can't believe it. She's a neighbor of ours," he went on to explain, "and as far as I know she has always been friendly to us. Tony certainly isn't their daughter, and if she's any relative of theirs, they should have claimed her long ago. I hardly think she has any real claim to Tony. Apparently she just wants to make trouble for us, although I can't imagine why."

He studied the matter, then said slowly, "I think the best thing would be to drive over and talk to Mrs. Manners right now. I like to handle things directly when I can. If Mrs. Manners really has justice on her side, then I want to make things right with her. But if she's simply determined to make trouble, at least we'll know where we stand. Come along if you want to, Ted. If I need your help later, it may be just as well for you to know as much about matters as you can."

The Manners farm was only a few miles away, which made them practically neighbors in their rural community. Mr. Fontaine pointed out their fields as they approached.

"They were planted this spring, but seem to be lying in a state of neglect ever since. I've heard that Mr. Manners has been having a good deal of trouble keeping his hired help."

When they knocked on the door, Mrs. Manners answered.

"Oh!" she exclaimed when she saw who it was.

"May we come in, Mrs. Manners?"

"Well, all right, but only for a minute," she answered ungraciously. "I'm very busy just now." She turned and led the way into the living room.

"Mrs. Manners," Mr. Fontaine began after they were seated, "I've come to talk to you about my daughter Tony."

"Your daughter?" said Mrs. Manners scornfully.

"Well, of course we've never made any secret about the circumstances. You know as much about that as I do."

"I don't see that there's anything about Tony for you to discuss with me."

"I shouldn't have thought so either until this morning when Mr. Kerch informed me that you had entered a demurrer objecting to our adopting her."

"Mr. Kerch has no right to say anything!" she answered shrilly. "He told me he would keep my name out of it if he could."

"Why would you want your name kept out of it, Mrs. Manners? Are you doing something you're ashamed of?"

"Certainly not," but she turned her eyes away.

"I'm sure, Mrs. Manners," said Mr. Fontaine, his quiet tone contrasting sharply with her raised voice, "that you must have some reason for objecting to our adopting Tony."

"Yes, I have." She flung her head up sharply. "Since Mr. Kerch has broken his promise to me, I'll tell you right now. I want Tony myself."

"But you hardly know her," he objected, very much puzzled.

"I've seen her quite a few times, and I've grown very fond of her. I mean to adopt her as my own daughter."

"But Mrs. Manners, if you felt this way about it, why didn't you do something about it long ago?"

"I have done something. I always intended in my mind that I would do everything I could to prevent you from adopting her, and now I have. You're one of those men, Mr. Fontaine, who has always been successful in everything you've tried to do. Well, this time it's going to be different. I've just as much right to Tony as you have, and I mean to have her. It's about time for you to learn that there are other people in the world who are entitled to a little happiness, too."

She looked wildly at them, until suddenly her spirit seemed to collapse, and she began to weep softly.

CHAPTER 5.

A VISIT TO HOP ALONG

It was obvious that Mrs. Manners had lost all control of herself, and Mr. Fontaine said soothingly, "I'm very sorry you've been unhappy, Mrs. Manners, but I can't believe taking Tony away from us will make you happy."

She did not reply, and feeling that it was useless to try to reason with her just then, Mr. Fontaine said, "Is your husband at home, Mrs. Manners? Perhaps if I could talk with him, we could straighten this out between us."

"No, he's been away for several weeks. But it wouldn't do you any good to talk to him. He feels exactly the same as I do about this. He wants to adopt Tony, too, and told me to go ahead. I think you'd better leave now."

At the door they said good morning, but she did not respond, and closed the door heavily after them. Slowly they walked to the car and got in.

"That certainly was queer," Mr. Fontaine remarked. "I never expected anything like that. I suppose she hasn't been feeling well, but that hardly accounts for such an outburst. I'd ask my wife to stop over and see her, but that would be a pretty presumptuous thing to do, as long as Mrs. Manners is trying to get Tony away from us."

"Do you think she can do anything, Mr. Fontaine?"

"If she has any real claim to Tony, she certainly didn't say so. I imagine she can't do anything except cause us a lot of trouble. But I don't like it, especially right now. Tony is about old enough to understand something of what's going on."

"I thought that Mrs. Manners might be jealous because your farm seems to be so much better than theirs."

"That might be part of the trouble. Actually, their land is just as good as ours, if they would build it up and take care of it. But Mr.

Manners isn't a farmer or rancher by trade. I believe he inherited this farm, and he's never quite made a go of it. He seems to be always flitting about, set on one get-rich-quick scheme or another. I don't suppose Mrs. Manners has had a very easy time of things."

"I didn't see anyone around, Mr. Fontaine. Is she trying to run that big farm herself?"

"The way things look, it doesn't seem like anybody's running things. They're down to about three or four head of cattle, I believe. Mrs. Manners must be taking care of them, and that's about all there is. I feel sorry for these people, but if they can't take care of a farm, how do they expect to take care of Tony?"

As they approached their farm, Mr. Fontaine said, "Let's keep this just between ourselves, shall we, Ted? I'll have to tell my wife and Bob sometime, and I'll do it in my own time and in my own way. I want to pretend there's nothing wrong, at least until I've had a chance to talk with Mr. Manners. I doubt that he's as enthusiastic about this adoption as his wife is. At least I may be able to reason with him."

"Of course, Mr. Fontaine," Ted promised.

As they arrived, Bob and Nelson came out of the house, having just had breakfast. Bob apparently was happy that he had had a reasonable excuse for getting out of morning chores, and Nelson announced himself glad for a little extra shut-eye.

"Where did you go, Ted?" he asked.

"Oh, Mr. Fontaine was showing me some of the other farms around here," said Ted, which was true as far as it went.

Bob had work to do, but told them they could ride into Hopalong with him that afternoon, which he seemed to regard as a treat. Ted and Nelson helped out a little with the work when they could and tried to stay out of the way the rest of the time. In the middle of the afternoon they cleaned up and set out for town, with Bob at the wheel of his father's car.

"I've got some shopping to do, and that'll give us a chance to look around and see who's in town and what everybody's doing. Almost everybody that can comes in about the time the train's due. The bus comes in, too, not long after, and that often brings visitors." He spoke as though visitors for his neighbors would be almost as much of a treat as visitors for themselves.

"Where do most people around here do their shopping—I mean for things like clothing?" Ted inquired.

"Well, the general store has a pretty good selection, and it will order something for you if you want it. Of course a lot of people around here order from mail-order houses. That keeps them going from week to week, but once or twice a year most people manage a shopping spree at one of the larger cities or towns. Why?"

"Oh, I was wondering about those footprints we found near the plane."

"The footprints of a giant?" Bob laughed. "Well, anyway, a pretty heavy man."

"They had an odd shape and I was wondering if the person who made the footprints might have bought his shoes right here at the general store."

"Hm, it's possible," Bob admitted, "except that if anybody that heavy came into town, everybody would know about it. But maybe he isn't really as heavy as you think. We can inquire at the store if you want to."

After Bob had ordered the supplies he had come for, Ted asked about the shoes. The proprietor, Mr. Collins, tried to be helpful, but the more Ted tried to describe the queer shape of the shoes, the more confused Mr. Collins seemed to get. Finally Ted got out a pencil and paper, and as soon as he drew the pattern of the shoes, Mr. Collins said:

"Oh, now I know what you mean. Yes, I do handle shoes like that, or rather, they're more of a half-boot. They were unloaded on me some time ago by a fast-talking salesman who assured me they were going over well in other places. I don't know about that, but the style never caught on around here. Wait, I've got a pair to show you."

He brought out a pair, and Ted and Nelson saw at once that shoes like these could very easily have made the prints they had seen. The shoes were nearly straight on the inside edge, with an exaggerated curve on the outside. Possibly they were comfortable, but they didn't look like much.

"Is this the pair you wanted?" asked Mr. Collins hopefully.

"No, I didn't want them for myself. I was just wondering if you had sold a pair like that recently."

"I haven't sold a pair of them since—I think it must have been about two months ago," said the proprietor, putting the shoes away.

"Do you remember who bought them?" asked Bob.

"Certainly I do, because the notion came to me that nobody except José would ever buy shoes like that."

"Can you tell us what size he bought?" questioned Bob eagerly.

"Yes, I can do that, too. They were size eleven."

"Isn't that too large for him? He's not a big person."

"I know, I tried to tell him, but you know how hard it is to tell him anything."

The boys thanked Mr. Collins and left the store.

"José is a deaf mute," Bob explained to the others. "He can't hear, except maybe just a little, and he doesn't talk at all, though some people think he could if he wanted to. The fathers up at the mission school taught him to read, but most of the time he pretends he can't do that either. You can figure out how hard it is to get an idea across to him, especially if he doesn't want to understand."

"How much does he weigh?" asked Nelson.

"Nowhere near three hundred pounds. Probably not even half that much, dripping wet. You'd better give up this idea about a three-hundred-pound man. I don't think there is such a person."

"Then you think it was José who visited the wreck?" asked Ted.

"That's hard to tell. I don't know what he would have been doing around there. He surely couldn't have known that the plane was going to crash. But if he did just happen to be there, he'll never tell."

It was time for the train to come in, but Nelson begged off. "Look, do you mind if I stroll around the town instead?"

"Sure, you do that, Nel. Just walk right up and talk to anybody you please. Everybody's friendly."

Presently the local came chugging up the track, and there was considerable bustle around the unloading platform.

"Nothing but packages today, men," the station master announced in passing. "No passengers," he informed the next group he passed.

Jake Pastor was just entering the station as they left. He had come into town mounted, for he refused to ride in a car.

"You don't catch me in one of those contraptions," Ted heard him say to a friend in a car who made a jibing remark. "I had a car once, but I had to get rid of it. It balked every time it saw a horse!"

Then he went on in, and they could hear him inquiring urgently after a package. Bob grinned.

"Sometime there will be a package for him, and he'll be so surprised he won't know what to do. Hey, what's Nel doing across the street?"

Ted saw Nelson apparently engaged in a conversation with one of the local people. "Come on," said Bob with a groan, grabbing Ted's arm and pulling him across the street. He went up to Nelson, nodded at the other man, then drew Nelson quickly away.

"What's the matter?" Nelson demanded. "You said everybody was friendly."

"I meant everybody except José. I don't think he could talk to you if he wanted to, and I'm sure he doesn't want to."

"So that's José. I was wondering why he was listening to me so quietly, but I thought he was just being polite. Those people laughing at me? You can tell them, Ted, about the time I ran eighty yards against North Ridge."

"I don't think they'd be interested," Ted answered. "Did you notice something about José? He *wasn't* wearing that type of odd-shaped shoes he bought at the store."

A friend a little older than Bob pulled up in his car, and Bob introduced his guests. The driver was Larry Kirstead, and he apologized for not getting out of the car because he was pressed for time.

"I hope you're putting these fellows to work for you, Bob. That's what I'd do if I had them up my way."

"You running short of help?"

"Sure, but who isn't, this time of year?"

"Losing any more sheep?"

"Wait a minute, what do you think this is? We don't lose one *every* night. Even a mountain lion doesn't get that hungry."

"Do you think there's a mountain lion?" Nelson inquired.

"Well, I tried to convince my dad there was, but he wouldn't give me the day off."

After Larry had driven off, they went on to the bus depot. When the bus pulled in, a number of people got off, none of them of any special interest to Bob. But he had a good time talking with the people around him, and introducing his friends. As Bob explained, they might never see any of these people again—unless it turned out that they needed them, and then everyone would be right on the spot to help.

They were nearly home again when Bob remarked, "Oh, nuts, we'll have to go back to town."

"What did you forget?" asked Ted.

"A present for Tony. I always bring her something when I go to town. She'll be disappointed."

"I've got a little shaving mirror I don't need," Nelson recollected. "Maybe she'd like that for her doll. Would that be good enough?"

"That sounds fine, and it'll save us an extra trip besides. She'll be pleased with anything."

When they drove into the farmyard, Tony came running to meet them. "Bob, I earned another nickel today. Will that help us go on our airplane ride?"

"Everything helps. You just keep right on."

"Give me a horseback ride, Bob?"

"Well, only up to the barn."

She was lifted up onto his back. "I'm going to have a ride on Starlight tonight," she remarked.

"Is she?" asked Ted, then realized that Tony had hoped to get a promise from Bob while he wasn't listening.

"Is she what? A ride on Starlight? You are not."

This little exchange with Tony had given Nelson the opportunity to hurry into the house and get the mirror. He returned now, and managed to give it to Bob without Tony's noticing.

"Here, Tony—something I got for you."

"What is it?"

"It's a mirror for your doll. Doesn't she need one?"

"Yes, she does. I told her this very morning that she should learn to part her hair better and she said she didn't have a mirror. Now she'll have one all for herself."

Bob went on to the barn, Tony ran into the house, and Nelson returned to the car to bring in the packages. Ted Was about to follow him when a man stepped out of the bunkhouse. This was not one of the regular hired hands, who were already known to Ted by sight and nickname. The stranger was young with a light complexion, and bright and friendly eyes.

He immediately extended his hand. "Hello, there. You must be Bob Fontaine. My name's Henry Cox. Your father hired me this afternoon."

Ted accepted his hand, but explained: "My name's Ted Wilford. I'm just a visitor here."

"Oh, well, I guess it doesn't hurt for us to get acquainted. Do you know when we have grub, or should I say chow?"

"It won't be long now. I understand that Mrs. Jansen uses a dinner bell to call in stragglers, but don't ever wait for it."

"Thanks for the advice. Glad I met you," and the young man strolled off whistling.

At the supper table Bob asked about the new man. "How's he doing, Dad?"

"Oh, you've met Cox? Doesn't know much about farm work, but he's a willing worker. I imagine he's an office clerk who wants to work outside for a while for his health. We can use him for a while. I don't think he plans to stay long."

But Cox seemed to be completely healthy, Ted thought, and found himself growing vaguely disturbed for no very good reason. He knew that ranchers didn't inquire too closely into a man's background, but accepted him at face value, until they had good reason not to. Surely there seemed to be little reason to be suspicious of Cox. He was the good-natured, open type of person who disarms suspicion.

"I didn't see another car outside, Dad. Did he get a lift?"

"Apparently not. He must have walked out from town on foot."

No more was said, and only later did Ted recall that they had watched the arrival of both the train and the bus that day, and Cox had certainly not come in on either one, nor had anyone mentioned him in town. It seemed more likely that he had arrived from over the hills, picking up the road this side of Hopalong. If he had done that, he must have passed many other farms where he could just as easily have found employment.

Ted didn't like to be suspicious, yet he could not escape the hunch that Cox hadn't arrived there entirely by chance. There must be some purpose that had brought him directly to Fontaine farm.

CHAPTER 6.

THE CRY OF THE LION

The boys went riding again that evening. When Tony saw them getting ready, she asked of Nelson:

"Are you going to ride Humpty-Dumpty again?"

"Who's Humpty-Dumpty?" Nelson wanted to know.

Bob looked embarrassed. "No fooling, Nel, his name really was Blaze at first. It was only afterward that everybody started calling him Humpty-Dumpty, until they almost forgot about the other name."

"Then why didn't you tell me he was called Humpty-Dumpty?" Nelson demanded.

"Well, er, don't you think you'd rather ride a horse named Blaze than one named Humpty-Dumpty?"

Nelson understood now, and looked a little grim. It was clear that he had been given the slowest, easiest-to-handle horse available, and that the name Blaze had been used to hide that fact from him. Then he laughed.

"Of course if you really wanted a ride on Starlight—" Bob offered, by way of apology.

"No, thanks. Humpty-Dumpty suits me just fine."

Somehow none of the boys felt like riding up to the ridge again. But there was plenty that Ted and Nelson had not yet seen in other directions.

"Let's ride over to the Franton place," Bob suggested. "I mean where the Franton place was. Nobody lives there now."

"A haunted house?" asked Nelson hopefully.

"Afraid not. The house burned down a couple of years ago, and I don't think there's enough left to interest a ghost. It's got a big barn, though."

A hole in the ground where a house had once stood was hardly a stellar attraction, but the ride was pleasant, and on the way Bob had time to tell them a little about the tragedy which had struck there.

"Mr. and Mrs. Franton were newcomers out here. They were apparently a hard-luck couple. It looked as though they had failed at a number of things, and were now going to try their hands at farming. Dad sent me over here, soon after they moved in, to see if there was anything we could do for them. I spoke to Mr. Franton, who seemed a very pleasant person, and his wife waved at me from the doorway. They didn't have anything for me to do, so I rode home, and that very afternoon the place went up in flames. They both died in the fire. Apparently the oil heater exploded, and the flames spread so quickly they had no chance to escape."

They found they could not go into the barn if they had wanted to, for it was padlocked.

"There wasn't very much left," said Bob regretfully, "just a little furniture, some livestock, and an old car. There'll be an auction in a couple of days and everything will go. Maybe Dad will let me take time off to come over for it. An auction's kind of fun, even if you don't buy anything."

"Who feeds the livestock?" asked Nelson, nodding toward the barn.

"The animals aren't in there. They were taken off by farmers around here, and will be replaced in kind for the auction."

When they rode up to the gaping black hole with the charred stone foundations, they got an idea of the extent of the tragedy.

"I don't see how any furniture was left, after a fire like that," Ted observed.

"Oh, the furniture wasn't all in the house. Some of it hadn't been carried in yet, or else they decided to store it in the barn."

"Why an auction?" asked Nelson as they started on the ride home. "Weren't there any relatives to claim things?"

"Not that we know of. The license on the car was traced and their old address found, but they had only lived there a little while, and no one knew them any more. I guess they were the kind of people who never stayed in one place for long."

They arrived home at sunset. It turned out that Mr. and Mrs. Fontaine were going out for the evening to visit friends, and were taking

Tony with them. The hired hands, with their day's work done, either had driven off or retired early. Only one light showed in the bunk-house.

Bob helped stable Meadowlark and Humpty-Dumpty, but did not unsaddle Starlight immediately.

"Say, would you mind if I rode over to see Larry Kirstead? He wanted me to help him work on his radio."

"Sure, go right ahead," Ted returned.

"We'll make ourselves at home," Nelson added.

"You can put on television if you want to; we often get a pretty good picture out here if you fool with it long enough."

Then Bob was off.

"It sounded like he wanted to get rid of us," Nelson complained. "He didn't even ask if we wanted to go along."

"Maybe he wanted to ride, and didn't think we were experienced enough to ride after dark. Anyway, he doesn't have to make excuses to us."

"You and I could have gone in the car," Nelson pointed out. "But I guess you're right. We don't have to hang on him every minute, just because we're visitors."

They tried the television set, but the picture was so fuzzy that they gave up. There were books and magazines around, and a copy of yesterday's newspaper. These occupied them for a while, and then, as Bob did not return and the house remained quiet, they decided it would be a good time to write letters home.

"Did you know that Tony wasn't really Bob's sister—that they're trying to adopt her?" asked Nelson.

"Yes, Mr. Fontaine told me."

"I suppose they make a point of telling everybody, so no one will make a bad slip of the tongue. Bob thinks that Tony doesn't remember very much about how she came here, but she may—just a little. Can you imagine her parents doing something like that, Ted? I guess it takes all kinds of people to make the world."

"And all kinds of problems, too. We don't know what they were up against. Maybe there are circumstances that would explain it, even if they don't entirely excuse it."

Since Bob had told Nelson, Ted saw no point in refusing to discuss the affair, though he was careful to make no mention of Mrs.

Manners and her threat. When their letters were finished, the evening still seemed young.

"Why don't we begin working on that report for Mr. MacCafferty?" Ted suggested.

"I thought we'd wait till all three of us were together."

"Oh, well, I don't see any reason why we can't start. Bob can add his ideas later."

They discussed the accident for a while, finding they were pretty well agreed on the time, the angle from which the plane approached Sandy Hill, its altitude, and other details. Ted got these down on paper, in a rough fashion. Then they went on to the second part of the report, the expedition to Sandy Hill. They worked on this together, each thinking of details to include that had not occurred to the other.

"Are you going to say that those footprints may have been made by José?" Nelson inquired.

"No, that would be just a guess. We don't know how many hands this report is going through, so let's keep everything just as accurate as we can make it."

"A three-hundred-pound man, then?" asked Nelson.

"No, just a very heavy man."

Then a sudden cry shot through the air. Ted almost dropped his fountain pen as they got to their feet. The cry was repeated, an unearthly cry such as they had never heard before, long, wailing, and menacing.

"The mountain lion!" Nelson exclaimed.

"What makes you think so?" Ted inquired.

"Well, whatever it is, I never heard anything like it."

They listened intently, but the cry was not repeated, although Cougar, apparently locked in the barn, had begun to bark. There was no other movement they could hear, no alarm from the bunkhouse or among the stock.

"So that's it," Ted muttered.

"What's it?" Nelson demanded, determined not to be excited as long as Ted wasn't.

"Why didn't Bob want us to go with him? Why is Cougar locked in the barn? Why isn't somebody stirring down at the bunkhouse? Surely there must be somebody there."

"Oh." Suddenly Nelson laughed. "So you think that's Bob out there?"

"Yes, and probably his friend Larry. The men in the bunkhouse must be in on it, too. This is probably a pretty good joke to play on the tenderfeet."

"What do we do, rush outside and try to catch them in the act?"

"No, we probably wouldn't find them, and I suppose there is just about one chance in a thousand that it really is a mountain lion. Let's play it real cool, just as though we weren't paying any attention to it."

"It would be pretty hard not to pay any attention to *that*."

They were in a little study off the dining room, and figured they were probably visible to Bob and Larry outside. They could not undo the fact that they had jumped up at the sound, but now they sat down quietly and continued working on the report. When they were finished, they sat back and stretched, as though they were thinking about bed.

"What do you think they'll do now?" Nelson whispered.

"Oh, I don't think they'll let us off this easy. That mountain lion will have to come back."

It was time for bed, so they switched off the light and walked through to the kitchen, where they ate the sandwiches Mrs. Fontaine had left for them. Then, without hurrying, they walked upstairs. Hardly were they in bed and the light out when the cry came again, even more plaintive in the still air.

"I've got an idea." Nelson crept over to the window and opened the screen. He had one of his old shoes in his hand and threw it out. "Scat, scat!" he called, then returned to bed, as they muffled their laughter in their pillows.

That was not the end, for fifteen minutes later a rifle began to fire. The visitors sat up in bed. It was becoming an exciting show. Were they really missing something? But then the shots ceased, and about half an hour later they heard Bob arrive home on Starlight. When he finally came upstairs, he opened their door quietly, but getting no response, closed it again and went on to his own room.

At the breakfast table, Mr. Fontaine inquired how the visitors had slept.

"Oh, pretty well, thank you," Nelson responded. "There was an old cat hanging around outside the window. I threw my shoe out at it, and that seemed to help some."

"I thought I heard a few rifle shots, too," Ted added, "but I didn't know there was night hunting around here. Maybe I dreamed it."

Mr. Fontaine looked shrewdly at his son. "What were you and Larry up to last night, Bob? One of your jokes?"

"Oh, not really a joke, Dad," Bob protested, looking down at his plate. "I was hoping they'd back me up when I came to ask for the day off. Besides, I thought they'd enjoy a hunt more if they really believed there was a mountain lion."

"You might have got a hide full of buckshot for your trouble."

"Oh, the men knew about it, too."

Henry Cox came on the side porch and up to the screen door.

"Mr. Jansen sent me over with a message for you. He said to tell you that Daisy was dry this morning."

"Daisy?" asked Mr. Fontaine, puzzled. "She shouldn't be."

"No, that's what he said."

"How was she last night?"

"All right, I guess."

"No sign of illness?"

"I don't think so. He said that the way it looked, she must have been milked already before he got to the barn. He thought perhaps you'd done it yourself."

"No, I certainly did not. Well, tell him to isolate her for today, and let me know how she is tonight."

"Yes, sir."

Cox gave a friendly nod to the others, then turned and left. Cougar had been lying in the doorway of the dining room, but now got up and pushed himself out the screen door. The new hand must have fed him something the evening before, Ted decided. It appeared to him that while Cougar would bark fiercely at a stranger, he would make friends very easily.

"What do you think happened to Daisy, Dad?" asked Bob.

"I've got that all figured out. Your mountain lion sneaked into the barn and milked her." Mr. Fontaine laughed. "Oh, I imagine it was José who was responsible for both the milk and the sheep. It's true that he could get fed at the mission house any time he wanted to, and it's also true that we'd all be glad to give him what he needed if he would only ask for it. But there is a certain type who think it's wrong to beg, but all right to take what he needs. The thing that makes it worse is that it is so wasteful. In this hot weather he would have no means of preserving the meat, and so most of it will go to waste. Well, I'm not going to raise a big fuss about a little milk or an occasional sheep or old blanket off the line—" he nodded at his wife "—as long as it ends there."

They were finished eating, and he rose from the table. "OK, Bob, how soon will you and your friends be ready to start out?"

"Then we can go?"

"Do you think there's any possibility of a mountain lion?" asked Ted.

"No, not really, Ted. There hasn't been one seen in this area for many, many years. But then, you never can be sure. Wildlife has a way of drifting back sometimes in the most unexpected fashion, once vigilance is relaxed. I was young once, and even in those days we couldn't match the tales the old-timers told. Maybe nobody ever can, but anyway you can have some fun. And if you do get that mountain lion, please bring home more of the tail than Jake Pastor shows around."

While their lunch was being packed and the horses made ready, Bob looked over the report his friends had written, frowning as he read.

"I see where you think the plane was about five hundred feet up when it went overhead. It seemed to me it was at least a thousand."

"Would it have disappeared behind Sandy Hill the way it did if it had been that high?" Ted questioned.

"Maybe not if it was flying level, but I think it was descending. And you both seem to think that it simply passed out of hearing, but I believe that the engine was cut off, either intentionally by the pilot, or else through some error or malfunctioning."

"We didn't hear the engine sputter," Nelson pointed out.

"No, there wasn't any sputter."

Ted and Nelson looked at each other doubtfully. The report expressed their best judgment, but they realized that Bob was more accustomed to the outdoors than they were, and his views might be more reliable than theirs.

"You may be right," Ted admitted.

"Now don't change it," said Bob quickly, anxious not to press his point too sharply. "Remember what Mr. MacCafferty said. Let's just add my opinions, too."

Then their lunch was ready, and it was time to get the horses from the stables and set off.

CHAPTER 7.

AT THE END OF THE GULCH

Recognizing the signs of an all-day hunting trip, Starlight held her ears alert, and the big, strong muscles of her legs quivered. Meadowlark seemed somewhat less eager, while to Humpty-Dumpty this appeared to be just another day's work. But the boys were all getting to understand their mounts, and no one cared to change.

Bob had a rifle, but the others were unarmed.

"It isn't so important that we get the mountain lion, as that we find out if there really is one," he explained. "If necessary, we could get a big party together and smoke him out."

Ted and Nelson couldn't decide whether Bob really believed in the mountain lion or not. It seemed to be something more than a joke that he was playing on tenderfeet. Ted had the feeling that Bob badly *wanted* a mountain lion, so that he might have some chance of matching the stories told by the old-timers. This being so, they were willing to play along with the game, and show just as much enthusiasm over the hunt as Bob did.

"Don't mountain lions work the night shift?" Nelson questioned.

"Usually, but extreme hunger or some unusual circumstance will lead them to change their normal habits. Anyway, even if he is holed up for the day, we should be able to find his spoor, or the remains of a kill, or something like that."

"Do they ever lie in wait in a tree overlooking a trail, waiting to pounce on a victim?" asked Ted, recalling some movies he had seen.

"Don't worry. If that's what he's planning, you'll probably never see him, he'll take care of that." And with these hardly reassuring words the group set out.

They galloped up toward the ridge, but didn't race for they had a long ride ahead. Crossing the ridge with hardly a pause, they started downward. This was the end of the rich prairie land and the beginning of the forest. Occasional trees grew more numerous, forming thick clumps. Before an hour had passed, they were well into the woods. With the trail now rough and winding, they had slowed down to a steady walk.

"Dry as tinder," Bob remarked, as twigs snapped sharply beneath the horses' hoofs. "I hope we're not in for a burn this summer."

The prospect was a grim one. To Bob, who had grown up in these woods, it would be a real tragedy, and even his visitors would feel a strong sense of loss, remembering the beauty they had seen and the fun they had had.

"Is there any real danger?" asked Ted.

"Well, Jake Pastor says this is the driest summer he's ever seen, and he's been around a long time. I don't think it's one of his tall tales, either."

"What really causes most fires?" Nelson questioned.

"Matches, cigarettes, and campfires that aren't really out get most of the blame, rightly or wrongly, and when that happens everybody says the 'dudes' were at fault.

"Myself, I don't blame it all on the dudes," Bob went on. "I've seen local people who ought to know better acting more careless than the visitors. And there are other causes, too, that maybe no one can quite help. Railroads used to start a lot of fires, especially the early wood burners, but of course they usually denied it and tried to blame something else. They said that more fires were caused by the sparks from horses' shoes, but whether that ever really happened I don't know. Some people even say that old bottles left on the ground will sometimes focus the sun's rays on dry leaves or needles or grass and touch off a blaze. Lightning is probably the most important natural cause, though a storm usually produces rain that puts out or limits the fire. But a severe electrical storm coming after a long dry spell could do it."

"I've heard it claimed that a lot of these fires are started deliberately," Nelson observed.

Bob's face grew long. "I hope not. I wouldn't want to believe that about anybody. Most of the suspected cases I've heard about were never proved."

"But I suppose some people get a feeling of importance out of destroying something," said Ted thoughtfully.

Game was neither so plentiful as earlier, Bob told them, nor as scarce as he had expected. Squirrels and rabbits were seen in fair numbers, but Bob's rifle was never raised even for a "sight." Under Bob's direction they studied each suspicious ledge, scanned each low, overhanging limb or nearby cliff, studied the dust for tracks, and watched their horses for unexplained nervousness.

To ride directly to Rainbow Gulch, and home again, would have made their day too short, and Bob proposed that they explore several other gulches along the way, saving the best for last. Dead Man's Gulch was their first objective, and Bob told them that it had been named for a young pioneer who had been found there with an arrow through his back.

"Some people say that he rode off on his wedding day, running the gamut of attacking Indians, in an effort to save the settlement. Other people say he was a traitor who was deliberately stirring up trouble by selling weapons to the Indians, playing both sides until simple justice caught up with him. I don't know which story is right, and I guess the people who named this gulch couldn't decide, either."

The first gulch was not too promising. The hillside was wooded, with few traces of the rocks which they felt were more likely to appeal to a mountain lion. Besides, it was too close to civilization, too open to intrusion.

"They say if you want to go hunting, you have to figure out what you would do if you were the animal you're after," Bob remarked.

"I want some raw sheep meat, gr-r," Nelson growled, and they laughed.

"Seriously, though, I think what a mountain lion would like is a nice cool cave," Bob decided, for the day had grown pleasantly warm. "That means we're out of luck here."

Although it was still early, they decided to stop for lunch. Afterward they set up a target, and fired at it for a while, so that at least they might have the satisfaction of saying they had used the rifle.

"Not that I'm going to take a chance on getting caught with any illegal game," Bob pointed out. "José is the only one who can get away with that. He seems to spend quite a bit of time around here, in season and out. The game warden tries his best to explain about licenses and hunting seasons, but he can't seem to get it into José's head. I guess sometimes there are advantages in being deaf."

"A lucky thing there's no closed season on mountain lions," Nelson remarked. "I can see where a mountain lion would explain the missing sheep, but then what about the cow that was milked? You got any ideas, Ted?"

"Oh, I could probably think of half a dozen if I tried."

"Go ahead, then."

"Well, it might have been Henry Cox," Ted explained slowly. "He's a green hand. Maybe he wanted to practice milking while none of the other men were around, and later, finding he had stirred up some trouble, he hadn't wanted to admit it."

"Not very good," Bob objected. "He'd know we use milking machines."

"Well, I didn't promise it would be very good," said Ted with a laugh.

The next two gulches yielded nothing, though they explored them as thoroughly as they could.

"So I guess it's Rainbow Gulch or we're out of luck," Bob announced. "And when we get there be ready for a surprise—if somebody hasn't tipped you off already."

They had been traveling rather steadily uphill most of the day. Now the woods were beginning to thin out as they reached the rocky uplands. As they turned into Rainbow Gulch, Ted and Nelson saw that it had all the characteristics they had thought would most appeal to a mountain lion: water, ledges, caves, seclusion, and accessibility both to the natural game of the woods and the not-too-distant farms when the natural food supply failed.

Ted and Nelson had not thought of inquiring how Rainbow Gulch got its name, but they knew as they made a turn and saw a natural bridge stretching out across the chasm above their heads. It was a scene of startling beauty. Once the bridge must have been a solid rock, but seeping water had created a hole which grew through the centuries, until the bridge rose to its present majestic arch from cliff to cliff. Its strata presented a myriad of colors, and particularly in the early summer when the sun set in the northwest directly behind it, they could imagine that it rivaled any of the natural wonders of the West.

"How'd you like to climb over the Rainbow?" Bob challenged.

"Has anyone ever done it?" Ted inquired. He recognized that it would be a tough climb, with loose rocks slipping beneath one's feet, and that coming down might be even worse.

"Oh, yes, I guess all the older boys around here have. Our parents warn us not to 'until we're older,' but they keep their fingers crossed, knowing that we will. I climbed it with Larry, but as far as I know no one has ever done it without a partner and a rope."

"You only did it once?" asked Nelson.

"Sure, we proved we could do it, so why risk our necks for nothing?"

With some reluctance they passed under the bridge and pushed on up the gulch. Unlike the previous gulches, with their long slopes of thick grass, here the grass was scant, and the sides steep. Points of rock jutted out precipitously. The trail was little used, for visitors seldom went beyond the Rainbow, and the valley looked desolate. A small, sparkling brook ran through the gully and they had to cross and re-cross it repeatedly.

This was the longest of the gulches, and turned many times. As each new view opened before them, they studied it eagerly for any signs of a mountain lion's hiding place, but without discovering anything definite. On one of these occasions Nelson said suddenly:

"Hey, does anybody smell smoke?"

It seemed that their horses did at least, for Starlight was unusually alert to her master's wishes, and Meadowlark seemed apprehensive. Only Humpty-Dumpty looked as though nothing would bother him.

Bob sniffed the air. "Yes, I think so."

"I hope it's not a forest fire," Ted remarked. "This could be a terrible place to be trapped."

"I don't think it is. It's more likely a campfire."

"Who'd be camping in here?" Nelson demanded.

"I don't know. It's coming from up ahead, I think. Let's take a look."

They advanced cautiously, until, after making another turn, a small spiral of smoke could be seen ahead. Bob drew rein, and the others came up to his side and halted.

"I don't like the looks of this," said Bob in a low voice. "It may be perfectly all right, and then again, it may not. It's certainly a queer place for anyone to camp out."

"What do you think we'd better do?" asked Ted.

"I don't think we ought to barge right ahead without knowing what we're getting into. Tell you what, let's try a flank attack. We'll go back until we can find someplace to climb out of here, tether our horses, and creep up on foot from above, until we see what's doing."

This was agreeable to the others. They turned back, and had to go some distance, back under the bridge and nearly to the mouth of the gulch, before finding a slope that the horses could climb. They made their way to the top, which brought them to a flat, grassy tableland, and here they dismounted. Making their horses fast, they advanced once more toward the wisps of smoke.

Below them the gulch made its serpentine curves, but above they did not have so far to go. As they finally neared the edge of the hill at the head of the gulch, they dropped to their hands and knees and crept forward. Below them, much to their surprise, they saw a battered old cabin.

"Do you see what I see or am I dreaming?" asked Bob in wonder. "I never knew there was a cabin there."

"It's a cabin, all right," said Nelson.

"I can see why you never suspected it," Ted observed. "It's set back so that you'd almost have to stumble over it before you came across it down below, and I imagine it's invisible from most places on the hills. It was only the smoke that led us to it."

"But that must mean someone's living in it!" Bob exclaimed. "From the looks of things, I'd say he's been living here a long time!"

"There's a path going down," Nelson indicated. "I'll bet we could creep down almost to the cabin without being seen. Let's try it and see what we can find."

The path was steep, but with many bushes on its sides which they counted on to shield them from view. They were able to get within a hundred feet of the cabin without being discovered.

"Listen!" Bob cautioned. "The door's opening. Someone's coming out. Down, and quiet."

Suddenly an old man stepped into view. His face was covered with white whiskers, his hair was unkempt, his shoulders slightly bowed as though by the weight of years or insurmountable troubles. He was carrying a water pail, and headed toward the spring. He passed within a few yards of their hiding place, and they could hear him muttering to himself.

The hermit—for there seemed no doubt that that was what he was—filled his pail and headed back for the cabin, again passing quite close to them. He disappeared inside, and though they waited some ten minutes longer, there was no further sign of him.

"Should we try to get closer and see what's going on inside the cabin?" asked Nelson in a whisper.

"No, let's get moving out of here."

Bob led the way back up the hill. Once out of sight of the cabin, they straightened up and made their way back to the horses.

"We certainly know one thing for sure," Bob pointed out. "There's no mountain lion in Rainbow Gulch. A man and a mountain lion can't live that close together. One or the other has to go."

"You think this explains the sheep and the milk?" Ted questioned.

"I'm sure of it. Look how it fits in. The only time things were taken was when natural game was too hard to get, during the winter storms or the summer drought. A hermit's like a clever mountain lion—he wouldn't want to get men on his trail, either."

"This is the screwiest thing I ever saw," Nelson decided. "I wonder how long he's been there?"

"Not as long as the cabin, of course, but I imagine he's been here for years. He looks completely settled in. You'd have to ride all the way into the gulch to find him, and no one's likely to do that. We only did it, at first, because we were after a mountain lion. Then if he was careful with his fires, and never came out except very late at night, who would suspect?"

"His clothes didn't look too bad," Ted recollected, "and he surely never showed up in town to buy them."

"But who is he, and what's he doing there?" Nelson persisted. "And why didn't you want us to take a peek in the window? We might have found out something. I don't think it would have hurt anything—he didn't look dangerous."

"I think I know what he's doing. He's a prospector of some sort. I imagine he thinks he's discovered something, or about to discover something, and that's why he's holed up there."

"What could he be prospecting for?" asked Ted.

"It could be almost anything—gold, silver, copper, maybe even diamonds or uranium."

"Don't things like that take a lot of equipment nowadays? He didn't look as though he'd have very much along that line."

"I suppose they do, if you want to do a really efficient job. But you still have some of these lone prospectors, hoping to stumble across something valuable. The way he walked and the way he muttered to himself made it look as though he's not quite right. That's why I didn't want to go bursting in on him. You don't know what notions he might take if he thought we were spying on him and going to beat him to his claim."

"You were the closest to him when he passed us, Ted," Nelson pointed out. "Did you catch what he was muttering about?"

"I'm not quite sure," said Ted, frowning, "but to me it sounded as though he was saying over and over to himself, 'Maryland, Maryland!' "

CHAPTER 8.

THE OTHER MAN

It was decided on the way home that Mr. Fontaine would have to be told about the hermit.

"I feel sorry for him," said Bob soberly, "and I'd like to let him alone as long as he wasn't hurting anything. But we can't go on losing sheep and other things. Besides, he might be in need of help. Getting through the winter might be tough for him."

"Wouldn't he need a gun if he was going to support himself?" asked Nelson.

"Not necessarily. Some of those older fellows are pretty clever with snares and things, though it's getting to be almost a lost art."

"What do you think about his clothes?" Ted questioned. "They would have to be replaced from time to time."

"Well, we don't know how long he's been there. He might have had a pretty good stock before he moved in."

Ted thought that would require forethought, and it didn't seem to him that this dazed man was capable of such planning, or of carrying on a systematic search for minerals, or of even knowing what to do with it if ever he had discovered something of value. Of course it was possible that he had been more clear-headed when he moved there, but if so, would he not have made plans for a better way of living for himself, and a better, more scientific method of prospecting?

And who was this man, anyway? Surely he was no one known to the neighborhood or he would have been missed, and quite probably a search made for him. But if he was a stranger, what had brought him here, and was anyone looking for him? Surely he must have been there for many months, or even years. Almost without thinking, Ted had agreed with Bob on this, and as he thought back he could recall the well-worn path between the cabin and the spring, some amateurish attempts at repairs to the cabin, and even a few vines strung up along the side of the house. This seemed to be about as much as the hermit was capable of. And—yes—to steal a sheep once in a while when hunger drove him to it.

At the supper table Mr. Fontaine listened carefully to their story. When they had finished, he had to agree with Bob that the mystery of the disappearing sheep had been solved.

"I didn't really think it was José—it was just that I couldn't think of any better explanation. But José, even though he might help himself to little things he needed, would hardly take a sheep. He would know better than that, and wouldn't want to get himself in trouble. I agree with you, Bob, that we ought to look in on the hermit before winter to make sure he isn't in need. Meanwhile, he doesn't seem to be doing much harm."

"There was a call for you this afternoon, Bob," his mother informed him. "Mr. MacCafferty is stopping out tonight for your report. I told him I wasn't sure how far along you were with it, but he is going to be out this way anyway."

"Ted wrote it up, Mom, and it seems to be in pretty good shape. There's a typewriter you can use to copy it on, if you want to, Ted. I'd do it myself, but it would be hunt-and-peck, and I wouldn't get done before midnight."

"Oh, I don't mind typing it," said Ted, "as long as both of you are satisfied with it."

Nelson said he was, and Bob that he would be, if Ted added the few small things he had suggested. After supper Bob and Nelson went out to the barn, for Bob had chores, and Nelson was developing considerable interest in farm machinery. Ted went alone into the study. He took out his fountain pen to correct the report before typing it and then turned to the typewriter. But before he was finished, Mr. MacCafferty had arrived and was shown into the study.

"I'll be through in a few minutes, if you don't mind waiting," said Ted, as Mr. MacCafferty sat down.

"Oh, no, not at all," said the CAP man obligingly. "If you've no objection, I'll read what you've written so far."

He read through slowly and carefully so that he finished studying the report very shortly after Ted had finished copying it.

"I think you've done a pretty good job," he announced, folding the papers carefully and placing them in an envelope in his pocket.

"It helps to get all these details down on paper before you forget what you really did see."

"I only hope it's of some help to you," said Ted, closing the typewriter and turning to face Mr. MacCafferty.

"It probably will be, although that's hard to judge at the beginning of an investigation." He crossed his legs and leaned back, as though doing some careful thinking.

"Have you learned anything more about the accident?" Ted questioned.

"Well, yes, in a way. I've done some checking into this man Jeff Leonard. He owned a farm downstate. He seems to have been the unscrupulous sort of man who would be willing to do almost anything as long as there was enough in it for him. Whatever he may have been up to this time, there's a good chance it was to no good."

"Then he did make an unauthorized stop?"

"Yes, there's no question about that. I believe I also have a good idea as to where he stopped. There's a big, empty field on his farm which would accommodate a plane of that size, so I imagine that was where he landed. Your report, showing the direction from which the plane came, helps to substantiate this."

"Do you know yet why he stopped?"

"I have a hunch about that," said Mr. MacCafferty deliberately. "I didn't mention it to you while we were at the scene of the crash, but there was some photographic equipment aboard. It seems to me more than likely that the plane was on some sort of photographic expedition. This equipment is expensive, and Leonard wasn't wealthy, but possibly he borrowed or rented it somewhere. Now I don't know whether or not this equipment was on the plane when it left the airport, but I suspect it wasn't, and the stopover was made for the purpose of installing it. It takes some skill to operate equipment of this kind, and I'm not sure Leonard could do it. But here's something I do know. He couldn't have used this particular equipment while he was piloting a plane. It would take another man to handle it."

"But there was only one man on the plane!" Ted cried.

"Was there?" asked Mr. MacCafferty pointedly. "Then how do you account for the fact that several pictures of Sandy Hill *were* taken before the crash?"

"Well, there was only one man when the plane left the airport, and there was only one in the wreck."

"Have you forgotten those footprints, Ted?"

"Oh!" For some reason it had never occurred to Ted that the footprints might have been made by a passenger in the plane. "But if he was in the wreck, wouldn't you suppose that he would have been injured, too?"

"Ordinarily you would think so, but it doesn't always work out that way. It's quite possible that the pilot could have been killed in the wreck, while his passenger was only shaken up."

"Then you think that this—this giant who made the footprints was originally on the plane?"

Mr. MacCafferty smiled. "I'm afraid that that giant exists only in our imaginations, Ted. Oh, I admit that you found footprints of a man who seemed to weigh more than three hundred pounds. But you've been thinking in terms of wild animal tracks. Let's think in terms of a domesticated animal, let's say a horse. Now what do you think?"

"Oh," said Ted thoughtfully, "I think I understand now. You mean a horse might be carrying a burden." He recalled that Bob and Mr. Fontaine had been skeptical about the weight of the man right from the beginning.

"Exactly. Footprints of a three-hundred-pound man might actually mean a two-hundred-pound man carrying a one-hundred-pound pack. Now we have to consider what was so valuable that a man, who had undoubtedly been severely shaken up in the wreck if not actually injured, should have carried it away."

"Any ideas about that, sir?"

"No, I'm stumped there. As far as we can tell there's nothing missing from the plane. Possibly it was something else that was loaded on the plane at the farm, where the photography equipment and the passenger were taken on."

"But if someone did leave the plane, where is he now?" Ted questioned.

Mr. MacCafferty stared at him quietly without answering, and Ted recalled that the prints had seemed to lead away toward Rainbow Gulch.

Could the hermit have been the man on the plane? Almost as soon as the idea occurred to him, Ted dismissed it. Unquestionably the hermit had been holed up in the cabin for considerably longer than two days. That queer, demented man was not sufficiently alert to participate in any scheme with Jeff Leonard, could not have handled the delicate photographic equipment. And it would have been a most remarkable coincidence if the plane he was riding in had just happened to crash a few miles from the cabin he was occupying. No, the passenger was definitely not the hermit.

Then could it have been José? Ted had to admit that, like Mr. Fontaine, he didn't really suspect José, but only thought of him because he couldn't think of anyone else it might have been. It couldn't, for example, have been Henry Cox, almost the only other name that came into Ted's mind. Cox was too much of a dude to wear those awkwardly shaped shoes; and though he might have put them on as a clever dodge, he surely couldn't have known in advance that the plane was going to crash, and that he would be leaving footprints in the mud in the dark.

So Ted was back to José again, and the slender clue of the odd-shaped shoes was the only evidence he had to support the idea. As for the depth of the prints, José was a slightly built man. Could he have carried something from the plane sufficiently heavy so that he made those deep prints? If so, what was it he had carried away, why did he want it, and where was it now? Wouldn't this be something more than the "light" stealing José was known to do? And Ted recalled, too, that they had seen José the next afternoon in Hopalong, and he showed no traces of the crash, which would have meant a miraculous escape. Ted would have liked to cross José off the list, except that if he did, there was no list left!

Mr. MacCafferty smiled, as though watching the inner workings of Ted's mind. "Then you can't think who the passenger is, Ted? That isn't so remarkable, for he might be a complete stranger. But as you say, what happened to him afterward?"

"Could he have been more badly injured than he realized, and died later out in the woods?"

"Possibly, Ted, but remember that he was probably carrying a very heavy object. Would an injured man be likely to do that?"

"No," Ted agreed, and laughed. "That would take us right back to a three-hundred-pound man, wouldn't it?"

Mr. MacCafferty smiled, too, as he rose to his feet. "Yes, very often logic does seem to lead us right around in a circle. By the way, Ted, you may be interested to know that we are ascribing the accident to 'pilot failure.' As far as we can tell, the plane was in perfect operating condition. It seems that the pilot in his inexperience must have made some important mistake. Probably he was more intent on getting pictures than he was in observing proper flying procedures. But just why he was taking photographs of Sandy Hill, and why he preferred to take them at twilight, are questions we'll still have to answer."

But Ted thought that the second of these questions, at least, was already answered. Leonard hoped to get his pictures in secret, and twilight seemed the best time, if he did not have infrared equipment for taking pictures in the dark. Dawn was another possibility, but you couldn't count on that in a countryside with early risers, and it would probably have led to further complications with the airport, for he had to call in just as soon as he could to make his explanations.

Ted walked out with. Mr. MacCafferty to his car, and watched him drive off. Returning toward the house, he ran into Tony. It was nearly dark, and time for her to be inside.

"I thought you were playing with Cougar," Ted remarked.

"I was, but he went off with that new man. He likes him."

"Mr. Cox?"

"Yes, he's nice. He was helping me teach Cougar some tricks."

Farmers are particularly rushed just before dark as they try to get as much done as possible, leaving only the least necessary things for the next day. Why had Cox taken time to play with Tony and Cougar at that hour of day? Surely it must have meant neglecting some of his other duties.

"Then you like Mr. Cox?"

"Oh, yes. He's nice to talk to. He asked me all kinds of questions."

Ted frowned. He had an idea that the Fontaines would not care to have Cox prying too deeply into their affairs. "What kind of questions, Tony?"

She became vague. "Oh, about if I liked living here, and what was my dolly's name, and things like that."

His questions seemed harmless enough, but Ted didn't like it. He wondered just what Cox had been fishing for, and then remembered about their unusual experience that day.

"Did he ask about the hermit, Tony?"

She stopped to think. "No." Then she went on in a moment, "But I told him all about it anyway."

For of course the subject had been discussed quite openly at the supper table, and Tony had been listening. Ted wondered now if that had been wise, though neither Bob nor his parents had seen anything wrong in it at the time. Were they going to spread the story around? They might rely on the good sense of their friends in staying away from the hermit until it came time to help him. Surely westerners would know enough to avoid a bewildered old man who was guarding some make-believe claim. But now Cox had the story, too. Would he have sense enough to stay out of it?

Tony went on into the house, and Ted walked toward the barn, intending to join Bob and Nelson. As he passed the bunkhouse, Mrs. Jansen called to him from the door. She was holding a sheet of paper in her hand.

"Is this yours, Ted? I found it on the ground, and I thought it might be yours, because I understand you're a newspaperman."

Apparently she thought that journalism was full of all kinds of secrets, and the paper she gave to Ted was as mysterious as any he had ever seen. He looked it over thoughtfully.

"Why, no, I've never seen anything like this before."

"Neither have I. That's why I thought it might be valuable. Last spring I burned up some of the men's checks, and had so much trouble about it that I've been very careful ever since not to burn something that might be important."

"It's just as well to be careful. But it isn't mine, and I don't know what it is or whose it could be."

"Then would you mind giving it to Mr. Fontaine? Maybe he will know."

"Yes, I'll do that, Mrs. Jansen. Thank you."

Ted walked on, studying the paper. He discovered that all the letters of the alphabet were to be found on each line. It certainly suggested some type of code, but he had no idea what kind. When he asked Mr. Fontaine in the barn, he was equally stumped, as were both Bob and Nelson.

"Why don't you take charge of it, Ted?" Mr. Fontaine suggested. "I rather imagine it is more in your line than mine."

Then Ted folded the paper and put it in his pocket, intending to see what he could make out of it later.

CHAPTER 9.

TEE AUCTION

With so many problems on his mind, Ted again slept fitfully. The most spectacular of the events of the previous days was the plane crash, and the mystery of the missing passenger. But this was of little personal concern to him, other than the fact that he was one of the witnesses, which entailed certain obligations. The haunting sympathy he felt for the hermit up in Rainbow Gulch was something he could do nothing about, for there seemed no way he could identify or help the man.

Closer to home was the strange circumstance surrounding Tony's introduction to the Fontaine family, and the threat Mrs. Manners had posed to the expected adoption. He knew little of Mrs. Manners, her temperament or her character, but he could not agree with Mr. Fontaine that Mrs. Manners was merely intent on trouble. The scene at her farm convinced him that Mrs. Manners really wanted to adopt Tony, and would do everything she could to make it possible.

Nor could he dismiss it as an idle threat. In his newspaper experience he had run into people who were mostly inclined to bluster, and those who were mostly inclined to act. Mrs. Manners had neither blustered nor threatened the Fontaines directly; instead she had taken legal action. If a responsible lawyer had taken her case, it would probably mean that she *did* have some legal justice on her side, or at least a case worth arguing in court. The fact that she had tried to hide her actions from the Fontaines indicated that she was not seeking an out-of-court settlement.

Awakening quite early, Ted slipped downstairs and returned to his room with a magazine he had noticed earlier. It contained an article on prospecting from the air, and he settled down to read it. He learned a number of things he had not known before: that a measurement of the earth's magnetism would often disclose the presence of iron ore, and—where the reading was low—other minerals; that a counter to measure radioactivity was not only useful for locating radioactive materials, but low readings would also be useful for finding other things which might shield the earth's natural radiation; that electrical conduction, as in a military mine detector, was also widely used. Nelson awakened as he was nearly finished, and he explained some of the things he had uncovered.

"You think that plane was on a prospecting flight, Ted?"

"It might have been. Have you got a better idea? Maybe it was the hermit that put the idea in my head. There is such a contrast between the way he is probably prospecting, and the way it would be done with an airplane."

"Now wait a minute, Ted. If that plane was making a prospecting sweep, it might have had some valuable equipment on board. If a passenger survived the crash, and he left the plane carrying something very heavy with him, could it have been some of this special equipment you are talking about?"

"That was what I was considering," said Ted. "He might have had some important reason for this, and not only that the equipment was valuable because in that case he could have left it there until he was rescued. Maybe this equipment would reveal what he was after, and that was why he felt it necessary to conceal it. I don't know much about these devices, but I suppose they come in various sizes, and in various degrees of sensitivity."

There was a brooding silence for a few moments, until Nelson said: "You don't seem very sure of it, Ted."

"No, I can see some objections. I'm not sure that after a crash like that he could expect secrecy any longer. It was certain that he would be questioned and his activities investigated. What good would it do to remove some of the equipment, especially since the photographs remained?"

"Still the fact is that he *hasn't* been found, and he *hasn't* been questioned, Ted, so maybe he was right after all."

"Yes, that's so. You'd think that the natural reaction of a man who had escaped an airplane crash would be to stay there and await rescue, but he didn't. There was some reason why he had to get away from the plane before he was found."

"He may have been dazed by the crash, Ted, and not quite certain what he was doing. Or he may have been injured and in need of help."

"Still, it looks as if he did carry something away from the plane, and unless he is an extraordinarily heavy man to begin with, the thing he carried must have been heavy. I don't see how it could have been maps or data, or anything like that, because he could simply put these in his pocket and tell his rescuers not to touch them. Under those conditions, no one legally could."

"Unless he was afraid of someone going through his pockets while he was unconscious."

"Yes, but his actions in walking away from the plane don't suggest that he was seriously injured."

"Anything else, Ted?" asked Nelson, as Ted paused once more and seemed momentarily lost in deep thought.

Ted nodded toward the magazine he had been reading. "It doesn't seem to me that any of these instruments mentioned would have been used in quite the way this flight suggests. It appears to me that they would be used in making a wide sweep over a great amount of territory. Then if something promising was learned, the possibilities would be investigated more thoroughly on the ground. On such a preliminary flight, I doubt if there would be any great need for secrecy—planes are doing those things every day. You needn't tell anyone else exactly where you've been or what you discovered.

"This flight seems different. I don't think it was a preliminary flight. I think it was a *verifying* flight, that something *had* previously been found, and they were now winding up the details. The flight seemed to have Sandy Hill as its objective. It suggests to me having been some sort of map-making project."

"Wouldn't an aerial survey be a first step rather than a last one, Ted?"

"Yes, a sweep over promising territory, but not over such a local objective unless something had previously been discovered or suspected. My guess is that they had found something—something valuable—and that the highest degree of secrecy was necessary. They would want to locate this thing accurately from the air, one reason being to determine whether it was on federal or privately owned land. There would be completely different procedures to follow in each case."

"Are you thinking of getting mixed up in mineral speculations, Ted?"

"Not me! And for that matter, not anyone I know. You're probably right that it would still be a speculation. Suppose they had discovered a large deposit of iron ore, for example. They couldn't be sure how pure or how extensive it was without making a great many tests. I doubt that they could hope to make tests like that in secrecy. The normal procedure would be to lease or buy up the land, or negotiate a claim or rights with the government, and then make the tests. All that would take a lot more money than most people can afford to risk."

"All this still doesn't answer the question of what the passenger carried away from the plane," Nelson reminded him.

"No, and I'm afraid that stumps me. I can't even make a good guess, except that I don't think it was equipment and I don't think it was papers, but I'm sure it was very valuable."

"Ore samples, maybe?"

"But why would they have taken those along on the plane?"

"You getting anywhere with that code, Ted?" asked Nelson, pointing to the paper Ted had left spread out on the desk from the night before.

"No, I don't think I can do anything with it. I don't believe it's a code message. It's a code *table* used to write a message. But I don't have a message to read, so what good does it do me?"

"It's a funny thing for anybody to be carrying around, though, and it must belong to someone who's been hanging around this farm—unless it fell out of that airplane!"

Nelson finally got out of bed, and stretched as his feet touched the floor. "Going to the auction today?"

"Oh, is that what we're doing? Then I guess I'm going. And no remarks, Nel. If they think an auction's exciting, then it's exciting."

"No remarks," Nelson promised.

When they were on their way to the auction on horseback, Ted asked Bob, "Did the Frantons own their farm?"

"I don't know as I ever heard. Maybe they did, and that's why there's been all this delay in settling matters. After Mr. Franton and his wife died in that fire, it had to be determined if there were any heirs."

"How could they have bought the farm, if they were as poor as you say?" Nelson inquired.

"I suppose they could have put up a small down payment and taken out a mortgage. In a way, their poverty was responsible for the fire. That very morning Mr. Franton had been in town to purchase a new part for his oil heater. Whatever he was doing to it must have been wrong."

There were some twenty cars parked in the farmyard, and the auction was low spirited. The stock was the first to go, and most of it was not even available to see. A farmer would simply tell what he had taken off the farm, and offer a replacement from his present stock. Then the bidding would begin, and would usually end with the farmer himself buying back his own animals.

Like the boys, most of the spectators had come simply out of curiosity and neighborliness, rather than with any desire to bid. The furniture which was next displayed did little to enliven matters. It had been shabby to begin with, and the storage in the barn ever since the fire had not improved it.

"Three dollars!" Bob shouted as a chair was put up, and though he intended it as a joke, it backfired, for there were no further bids, and he found himself the possessor of a large easy chair which would require recovering if it was to be used.

"What's your mother going to say to that?" asked Nelson.

"I know exactly what she'll say. 'Put it up in your room.' Well, I need a chair, and I'm not fussy about styles."

A few more items were sold for small sums, though bidders were a little more wary after Bob's experience, and a small wagon brought only fifty cents. Then the battered old car went for a hundred dollars, and the sale was over.

"Weren't they going to sell the farm?" asked Ted.

"No, that wasn't listed." Bob motioned to the sheriff who was just passing. "Did the Frantons own this farm?"

"Oh, no. It's owned by Carl Manners. He bought it just a short time before the Frantons moved here."

"That's queer," Bob remarked, as the sheriff moved on. "I never heard tell that Mr. Manners had bought this place. I suppose he dealt with the absentee owners, and no one ever bothered looking up his deed. He's kind of a secretive person, always afraid somebody's going to find out what he's doing. But I don't know why he wanted a second farm when he doesn't take care of his own."

"Is this very good land?" asked Ted, looking at the neglected fields.

"Scrub," said Bob scornfully. "I wouldn't bother with it myself. Somebody could, though, who wanted to put a lot of time and money into it."

"Then how did Mr. Franton expect to make a living from it?"

Bob shrugged. "He couldn't. He would have failed with it, the way he failed with everything before. Maybe the farm sounded a lot better in the East than it looked after he got out here. If he expected Mr. Manners to fix things up, I think he was due for a surprise."

They rode back in a leisurely way toward the farm talking about many things. As they neared the farm, Bob suddenly drew up the reins on Starlight and pointed down into the dirt. Some footprints were to be seen, though they were not very legible. The boys followed along, departing from their normal trail. The prints led them toward the Fontaines' back meadow. Here they came to an end behind a series of bushes, and there was a great deal of trampling about, as though the man had been there for quite some time.

"Sort of looks like somebody was hiding here," Nelson guessed.

"Or that he was watching something," Ted suggested.

"If we could only find a really good footprint," said Bob, searching about. At last he called to them from some distance away, "Hey, look here!"

The guests rode to his side, being careful to avoid the print he had discovered. They studied it for several moments. It was pointed away from the meadow, suggesting that the man had been unable to get what he was after, and had finally left.

"Is it my imagination," said Nelson, perplexed, "or is that shoe really curved too much along the outside?"

"Are these the same as the footprints you saw on Sandy Hill?" asked Bob anxiously.

Ted looked doubtful. "They might be. They aren't very distinct, so it's hard to tell, but I'd say they're about the same size."

"You can't tell much about the weight of the man," said Nelson, having dismounted to look at the print more closely. "The ground is hard, with a little layer of dust over it. What do you think about this print, Bob?"

"Oh, I think it was probably made by José. That's about the way he would do things. He'd come here intending to pick up something, or maybe just to look around to see if there was anything worth picking up. I imagine for some reason he was afraid to approach the farm more closely, and finally left. I'll tell Dad about it when we get back."

Mr. Fontaine also believed that the footprints had been left by José.

"He has been caught taking small things, and I've no doubt he hasn't changed his habits."

"What was going on in the meadow, Dad, that he was afraid to come any closer?"

"Why, the goat was tethered there, and I believe Tony was out there playing with him most of the morning. Some of the men were keeping her in sight, and I suppose that was the reason José didn't come any closer. You're sure those prints weren't there very long, Bob?"

"They couldn't have been, or we would have ridden over some of them on our way to the Frantons'."

"By the way, has anyone seen Cox?" asked Mr. Fontaine. "I thought maybe he took a notion to visit the auction. I couldn't find him when I was looking for him."

"No, Dad, he wasn't there. Did you ask at the bunkhouse?"

"I was just about to."

The others rode along to the bunkhouse, where Mrs. Jansen came out to meet them.

"I haven't seen Henry Cox around," Mr. Fontaine informed her. "Has he been here?"

"Yes, he was. I understand he heard that Mike was driving into town, and decided to go along. I thought he had your permission."

"No, I didn't know anything about it. Of course he doesn't need my permission for every little thing he does, as long as he gets his work done. Do you know when he's coming back?"

Mrs. Jansen looked mysterious. "I don't think he's coming back. The only luggage he had with him was that little bag, and he took that with him when he left."

Mr. Fontaine shrugged as though he didn't understand, and probably didn't much care. At the lunch table, further mention was made of Cox's departure.

"I'm surprised that he would leave without telling us," Mrs. Fontaine maintained. "He was such a polite young man. And you owed him for a few days' wages, too."

"Maybe he didn't need the money," Mr. Fontaine remarked. "He must have been working at something before this, and it certainly wasn't farming."

"I saw Mr. Cox this morning," Tony spoke up. "He took my picture. I wanted to get dressed up first, but he said it didn't matter."

"How many pictures did he take, Tony?" asked Ted, his eyes narrowing.

"Two rolls," she answered, nonchalantly.

"Oh, you must be mistaken," said Bob quickly. "He wouldn't take two rolls of pictures of you."

"He did, too!" she asserted. "I know, because he finished one roll, and took it out of the camera, and put in the other roll, and finished that one, too."

The older people exchanged puzzled glances. It was easy to understand that Cox might want a picture of Tony, as a kind of souvenir of his stay at the farm, but why would he take two rolls?

"Well, I guess it was no crime for him to take your picture, Tony," Mr. Fontaine remarked, trying to remove any of Tony's doubts, though the grownups could not be so easily satisfied.

"Two rolls! Holy cow!" said Bob under his breath.

And Ted, who had had his suspicions of Cox before, was now even more puzzled over what Cox was up to, and wondered if they had really seen the last of the man.

CHAPTER 10.

FATHER WARREN'S COUNSEL

"I've got several errands this afternoon, Nel. Mind if I take your car?"

"It's all yours," said Nelson, handing the keys to Ted. "Sure you don't want me along?"

"You're welcome to come if you want to."

"Not necessarily, unless you need me. I think Bob and I have about got that old tractor licked."

"Then stick to your grease. I'll make out all right."

"You know," Nelson offered, "I don't think it's so unusual that Cox should take two rolls of pictures of Tony. I've occasionally done that myself, when I wanted to enter a picture in a contest, or something like that, and wanted to be sure that I got the best possible picture of my subject."

"That's right, but it does show something more than just a casual interest, doesn't it?"

"Undoubtedly. What do you think, Ted? Could this Henry Cox be a newspaperman?"

"I'd thought of that. He's certainly got one of the newspaperman's outstanding traits: curiosity. But I don't really think so. Usually a newspaperman lets everybody know what he is, and then goes around asking questions of anyone in sight. Cox acts as though he knows more than he's telling, while a newspaperman usually asks more than he knows."

Ted settled himself for a long drive. His destination was the city of Monroe, the county seat where the daily paper was published. If he was to help Mr. Fontaine, he felt it important to know just what kind of publicity Tony's story had received at the time . . . and while he was about it, he intended to fish around for a few other things, too.

Though the road was not heavily traveled, he got stuck behind a slow-moving drilling rig, and was unable to pass it for many miles. Probably intended for local use, Ted thought, or it would be traveling the main highways rather than one of these back roads. But he passed it eventually, and made better time after that.

At the newspaper office, he introduced himself to the editor, who had heard of Mr. Dobson's reputation.

"Is this a story for you, Ted?"

"No, I don't think so. I'm here on behalf of friends," and he went on to describe the incident of Tony's appearance.

"I'll turn you over to one of my assistants, and you can look up the back files. But I remember the story quite well. The situation is still the same, then? We run a story, and then if nothing new develops we drop it, and perhaps never hear about it again."

"Do you remember what sort of response that story received?"

"Oh, we got a few dozen letters, I think, some expressing sympathy, some asking questions or offering tips. Anything that looked at all promising we turned over to the police, but nothing ever came of it."

"Then I take it the story wasn't very widely publicized."

"No, I don't believe so. It would depend on each individual editor and how crowded his space was for that particular day. And you know enough about newspapers to know it's usually pretty crowded. We sometimes get complaints from readers, 'Look at all the space you're giving to junk,' but somebody wants to read that 'junk' or we wouldn't be publishing it."

After sending his regards to Mr. Dobson, he turned Ted over to the assistant who quickly produced the required files. As he studied the story, now two years old, Ted saw that his earlier expectations were right. In cold newspaper type, the story did not appear particularly sensational, nor was the photograph, probably secured under deadline pressure, as sharp as it might have been. Although the assistant did not know for sure, he expressed doubts that either Mr. Fontaine's name or the picture had gone out over the wire. Then the story became hardly more than a little filler, which a few papers might use but most would overlook.

"It's a little deflating, isn't it," the young man remarked, "to realize that something so important to you has such a little effect on the world?"

Ted also wanted to look up the newspaper story about the Franton fire, and found that it occurred within two weeks of the other story. Other than that, the small community of Hopalong seemed to get little publicity in the Monroe paper, though Ted searched back and forth through several months. It seemed that he had about exhausted the newspaper as a source of clues.

After thanking the editor and his assistant, he left the office. His way back took him in the general direction of Hopalong, but not straight to it. He had decided to stop off at the mission house where apparently José had received most of his help. He was not quite ready yet to dismiss José as the passenger on the plane, nor did he know yet just how much José could do and understand. Those prints found near the back meadow had aroused his interest. Bob and his father thought that José was not the passenger on the plane, but that he was the person standing by the meadow. Yet the general similarity of the prints suggested that they could have been made by the same person. If he could eliminate José as the passenger, he might also be able to eliminate him as the man at the meadow. This could mean . . . that the missing passenger was still hanging around.

Explaining his errand at the mission house, he was introduced to Father Warren, and shown into a quiet study.

"Although I'm a newspaperman, Father Warren, this isn't a newspaper story. I'm genuinely interested in helping my friends, the Fontaines, and in a way concerned, as I am sure you are, that José does not get involved in something more serious than he realizes. Yet it is hard for outsiders to judge just how much he does realize. I have heard some talk that he is exaggerating his defects, if not actually shamming."

"Exaggerating, Ted? I don't think that is quite the right word. He *can* hear a little, he *can* read a little, he *can* make a few sounds that a patient listener could interpret as words. But because he knows his abilities are limited, he distrusts them, and prefers not to use them. I'm sure you wouldn't want to play on a baseball team where all the other players were much better players than you, now would you?"

"No, I guess not, Father," Ted agreed. "But people believe that José will help himself to little things without asking, and I'm hoping that it hasn't gone beyond that."

"I've known José a great many years," said the priest warmly, "and I have great faith that he would not do anything he thought was very wrong. Stealing? I'm afraid that's true, but let's try to look at it as José sees it. We at the mission would do anything we could to help him, but he doesn't often ask, and we have found it a wise policy not to try to help a man more than he wants to be helped. He picks up jobs here and there, and I'm sure no one in the community would let him become destitute. It is perhaps that very feeling of charity which leads him to believe this really isn't stealing. He takes only small things, things which he needs and believes would hardly be missed, and would be given to him freely if he asked.

"But think how difficult it is for him to ask! It's not merely that it puts him in a begging position, but it also exposes his infirmities to public view. Have we a right to expect that of him?

"But I must agree that José is not wise in the ways of the world, and that he might be led to do something wicked by a stronger-minded person who assured him that there was nothing wrong about it. That is why I am interested to know just what it is that you suspect him of."

Father Warren sat back and folded his hands. Then Ted told him about the clue of the misshapen shoes, and how they related to the airplane crash and the footprints found at the meadow.

"Do you want my assurance, Ted, that José was not the passenger on that plane?" Ted nodded, and Father Warren went on: "Then I give it to you gladly and whole-heartedly. This is no longer a question of my faith in José, but what I know of his personality. He would never voluntarily ride in an airplane. He doesn't understand what keeps an airplane up, therefore he would be suspicious of it, and would reject all attempts to take him up. He would not care for the human relationship involved, with the pilot and others, and operating the photographic equipment you speak of would lie completely outside his competence."

"Thank you, Father," said Ted, rising to his feet. "I accept your judgment. I'm sure now that José wasn't on the plane. And either the man at the meadow was not José at all, or if it was, he was engaged in some activity which he considers harmless."

But José was *not* the man at the meadow, of that Ted was sure. It was the missing passenger, and whether he was merely in hiding or had some more sinister purpose in mind remained to be seen.

Ted's way home took him through Hopalong, and he found it was just about time for the train to arrive. There was a certain bustle and friendliness about the train's arrival that was beginning to tickle his fancy.

"Come along and have some fun," a man called to him as he parked the car. "Jake Pastor's going to get his package today."

The train pulled in, and Jake inquired of the station master about his package as usual while the group of spectators inched closer.

"Why, yes, Jake, there *is* a package for you. Just wait here and I'll get it."

No one could have looked more surprised than Jake did, but he waited expectantly for the package to be produced.

"Come on, fellows," someone called, "Jake's got his package. Let's see what it is."

The station master returned, and had Jake sign a slip before handing him the small bundle. Jake tucked the package under his arm and made as though he was about to leave.

"Well, fellows, guess I'll have to be hurrying along. Mighty important package, and I've got to get it home before anything happens to it."

"Oh, come on, Jake," someone coaxed, "open it and let's see what it is."

"Sure, Jake, you've got to let us see it. It must be pretty valuable, you've been inquiring about it for so long."

It was obvious that Jake was nearly dying with curiosity himself, so he allowed himself to be persuaded, and began to tear off the wrappings. Finally he lifted out an old-fashioned automobile horn from the heavy layers of tissue paper!

"What are you going to do with that, Jake? You don't own a car."

Jake was surprised but ready to carry it off. "Why, sure, it's just what I've needed. I'm going to attach it to my saddle, and make you fellows pull over to the side when I want to pass you up."

There was a good deal of kidding but gradually the group broke up. Then Jake spotted Ted, and called to him.

"Hi, there, what's-your-name, did that friend of yours find out what he wanted?"

"Which friend of mine?" asked Ted.

"That new man you've got out at the farm. I had a long talk with him this noon. He asked me all sorts of questions about early settlers and names of places and things like that. I figured he was either a nut or a writing fellow, and they're almost the same thing. Don't know what he was after, but I've been wondering ever since if he got it."

If Henry Cox wanted any local gossip, Jake Pastor was the right man to go to, Ted thought. Cox seemed to have an insatiable curiosity, though just what line it was taking Ted was at a loss to guess. But just then he was less interested in Cox's conversation with Jake than he was in the whereabouts of the man himself.

"Do you know where Cox went afterward?"

"Tried to get a ride, I guess, but I didn't see him after that."

Ted proceeded on toward home. He was about a mile from the farm when he noticed a figure up ahead, motioning with a thumb. As he came closer, he saw that the tired and dust-covered traveler was Henry Cox. He drew up beside him.

"Where do you want to go?"

"Back to the farm. I work there . . . I guess."

"I wouldn't be too sure about it. Mr. Fontaine seemed pretty put out with you when I left."

"Can't say that I blame him," said Cox cheerfully, getting into the car, "but he can't do anything more than kick me out."

"Well, be prepared. He knows about your taking all those pictures of Tony, and your pumping her for information about the hermit, and he's wondering about a few other things besides. But mostly I don't think he has much patience with a man who accepts his pay but neglects his work."

"You mean I've got to have a story ready that will answer all those things?"

"Why a story? Why don't you try the truth and see how it sounds?"

"Oh, I'm a firm believer in truth, Ted," said Cox with a laugh. "But the truth is such a big thing that everybody has to choose which parts of it he wants to tell."

They drove into the farmyard, and Mr. Fontaine happened to see Cox getting out of the car. He came over toward them. He was not a hasty man, nor did he believe in condemning a man unheard.

"I'm reporting back for work," Cox announced, "if I still have a job."

"That all depends. Where were you today?"

"In Hopalong. I had some pressing personal business, thought I could take care of it quickly, but it took me a great deal longer than I planned. Then I expected I could rent a car to bring me back, but nobody in Hopalong ever heard of such a thing, and when I tried to pick up a ride I found that nobody was leaving until that blinkin' train came in. So I decided to walk, until Ted picked me up about a mile down the road."

"I understand you had quite a conversation with Jake Pastor," said Ted.

"That was between telephone calls. I had to wait for an answer, and that was what took me so long."

"What did you do with those pictures you took of my daughter?" asked Mr. Fontaine.

"I mailed them away to be developed, as long as I was in town."

"Did you intend them for publication?"

"It might come to that eventually, but I would never do such a thing without your permission." He looked down at his fashionable, dust-covered shoes, then up directly into Mr. Fontaine's eyes. "Am I still working for you?"

Mr. Fontaine studied the man carefully.

"A few more questions first. Did you secretly milk one of my cows the other morning?"

"No, I did not." Cox's gaze was direct and unwavering.

"Do you know who did?"

"No, sir."

"Do you know who made those footprints up by the wrecked airplane?"

"No, sir."

"Do you know who that hermit in the woods is?"

"No, sir, nor am I much interested. As far as I know these woods could be filled with queer prospectors."

"Did you lose a paper with some queer lettering on it?"

"Yes, I did." Cox's face lit up. "I'd like to have it back, if I may. It's of little value to me, but I would prefer not to have it floating around."

"Can you tell us what the paper was for?" Ted questioned.

Cox looked at him, then returned to Mr. Fontaine. "Must I answer that question?"

"No, I guess not. Give him his paper, Ted."

Ted drew the paper from his pocket with great reluctance. "Would you mind describing it first, so I can be sure it's yours?"

"It has an alphabet along the top and down the side. If you find the letter V in each place, and trace down the lines to the point where they cross, you will find letter Z. Will that satisfy you?"

Ted checked and found that it was so, and restored the paper to its owner. Then Cox once more looked questioningly at Mr. Fontaine.

"All right, then, Cox, you're still working for me, but remember to tell me before you leave the farm again. I can only use men I can depend on."

"I'll remember. Thank you, sir," and Cox walked off, too jauntily to seem truly repentant.

CHAPTER 11.

THE SECRET WORD

Up in their room as they were cleaning up for supper, Ted had a chance for a private report to Nelson.

"It was probably a wasted day for me, but it's hard to tell at this point. I went to the newspaper office in Monroe to look over their back files, then stopped off at the mission, came back through Hopalong where I learned that Cox had had a long conversation with Jake Pastor this morning, picked up Cox on my way home, and arrived home with the gas tank about five gallons lower."

"Just what did you find out?"

"Father Warren convinced me that José wasn't the passenger on the plane, and that's about it, I guess. I'm no closer to knowing who the passenger was and where he is now."

"What do you think about Mr. Fontaine's taking Cox back on?"

"He's probably being more generous than I would be in his place. Still, if Cox really is on to something, it might be just as well to have him around where you can keep an eye on him.

"He certainly puzzles me, though, and yet I have to admit we don't have much against him. I suppose it's his own business if he wants to carry a code table around with him—though I wish now I'd kept a copy of it. He asked Tony some harmless questions, might have taken her picture to enter in a photography contest, maybe gabbed with Jake Pastor just because he likes to talk, could have had a perfectly legitimate reason for going to town today, for I can see why he wouldn't want to make long-distance calls from here. These are all little things, but how much do they add up to? The real thing I have against him is that he seems talkative enough but never talks about himself, and I don't know why he picked this particular farm at which to apply for work, the kind of work he isn't much suited for at that."

Ted was so busy talking that he actually bumped into the chair before he noticed it. "Well, I see they delivered it today."

"We drove over and picked it up. And Bob's mother said exactly what he told us she would say, down to the very words! But I asked her if we could have it for the guest room for a while, because there was only one chair here. I'm betting it won't be here an hour after we leave, though."

They had their ride after supper. Then Bob and Nelson went back to mooning over their beloved engine, while Ted went up to his room to read for a while—or try to read, for his mind kept wandering. Yet he was unable to come up with very much that he had not already mentioned to Nelson. He was convinced by now that the mysterious plane *had* been engaged in prospecting, but prospecting for what? He hadn't tried to pin it down more closely until recalling that long drive to Monroe stuck behind that drilling rig, it suddenly came to him: how about oil?

The more he thought of it, the more probable it seemed. An aerial survey was certainly a possibility, and there would be a need for privately acquiring leases before trying to interest one of the big oil companies in speculative drilling. But what about the hermit in the gulch? Was he interested in oil, too? This seemed a good deal less likely. Where were his maps, his testing equipment, how would he go about getting leases? One thing certain about oil was that you never knew what you had until your well was drilled and the oil either began to flow, or didn't. Though there might be a rare case of surface seepage, it wasn't ordinarily the sort of thing you found lying about on the ground.

The book in his lap was forgotten, and almost unthinkingly he slipped his hands down inside the cushions of the chair, a habit he had picked up as a boy when he often found small coins this way. He didn't find a coin, but he did detect a crackle of paper, and he gingerly slipped it out. It was a sheet of theme paper such as is often used in school, and there was a message on it, a message that did him no good at all, for it was in code!

He jumped to his feet. This was the time at last for a showdown with Henry Cox! He found him at the bunkhouse, his work done for the day, and invited him to step outside.

"Fists, swords, pistols, or pies?" asked Cox with a laugh, but he joined Ted by the fence out of earshot of anyone else.

"I'm hoping it won't come to that. I want you to give me back that code table—"

"Oh, I thought that was all settled, Ted. Since you weren't prudent enough to make a copy of it, then nothing doing."

"—in return for a code message."

"What!" Cox cried. "A code message! Where did you get it?"

"Want to go up to my room and talk it over? There won't be anyone there."

"You bet," Cox agreed, following him into the house and upstairs. After they were seated, he asked, "Now where did you find this code message?"

"Inside the cushions of the very chair you're sitting in. We got it this morning at the Franton auction."

"Nobody told me about any furniture. I understood there was just livestock going up, and an old car that apparently had already been gone over thoroughly, for they were trying to locate any possible relatives. I intended to search the barn later, though I didn't really expect to find it there. It seemed to me that the message was either in the house or carried by Mr. Franton, and in either case would have been lost in the fire."

"Then you're still interested in this message?"

"You bet I'm interested. What's the deal? A straight trade of my table for the message?"

"No, I don't think it's quite that simple. In the first place, I'd have to be sure that the table would be as useful to me as it would be to you. I'd have to know how to use it."

"That's easily taken care of, Ted. I can promise you exactly that, and nothing more. You can even be sure it will be the right table, for I haven't had time to prepare a faked one."

"Then, the second thing is that I would have to know that I was acting in the best interests of the Fontaines. I couldn't do anything that would be disloyal to them. That means I would have to know a little more about your background and what you're doing here. It's obvious that you have some connection with the Frantons, or you would hardly be so interested in a message found in their old chair."

Cox tapped on the desk as he meditated. "You drive a hard bargain, Ted. I admit I've been suspicious of you from the first, ever since I learned that you were a newspaper reporter. Newspapermen have a way of nosing into everything, and I wasn't sure whether publicity would be helpful to my cause or extremely harmful. Are you sure this isn't a newspaper story for you?"

"No, it's nothing of the kind. I'm willing to do anything that will help you, as long as it doesn't hurt the Fontaines."

"I believe you, Ted. As a matter of fact, one of my reasons for going to town today was to make inquiries about you. I had a number of things to call back home about, and your name came up. That may be the reason why my return call was so long delayed."

"What did you find out?" asked Ted curiously.

"About you, nothing, but a good deal about Mr. Dobson and the *Town Crier*. If you're an associate of Mr. Dobson, that's good enough for me. But you have your loyalty, Ted, and I have mine. If our loyalties do not conflict, we can be friends. Otherwise we will be opponents. Right now my loyalty is to a person whose name I don't even know, and for all I can tell may not even exist."

"That's a strange kind of loyalty," said Ted with a smile.

"It is, but we run into it quite often in my business. Let me explain who I am. My father was the attorney for the Frantons, and I suppose that now he is looking out for the interests of the heirs—if there is an heir, and if there is an estate. You can see what I mean about my loyalty being to a person who may not exist. I'm still in law school, and I work as my father's clerk. Have I told you enough so that you will trust me with the first five letters of the message? If so, I can explain how this table works, which is as good a place as any to begin."

Referring to the message, Ted wrote these five letters on a piece of paper which he put on the desk:

W M K T Y

Cox took the table from his pocket and spread it out on the desk. "This is called a Vigenère table, and you are correct that it is a code— or to use the more accurate term, a cipher. If you have any idea that we're going to be able to read this message right off, you can forget it. We're still lacking one important ingredient. Now let's imagine a secret word that was used to write this message."

"What sort of word would make a good secret word?" asked Ted.

"Well, it shouldn't be too short, and it's better if it has no repeated letters in it, and if it contains a letter close to the end of the alphabet. Just suggest something."

Ted thought rapidly. "How about 'Maryland'?" he suggested.

"All right, Maryland, though the A is repeated," Cox agreed. "We'll put the first five letters down like this."

W M K T Y

M A R Y L

"Now we use this table to combine letters. We find W on one of the normal alphabets, and M on the other, and see where they meet. Let's see, W and M gives us F. That's not bad for a first letter, so let's go on. M and A gives us I as a second letter. Things are looking up a little. Now K and R, and that gives us R. Our first three letters are FIR, which isn't bad at all. Now T and Y. That gives us L, FIRL. Not very good at all. I think we've had it, and it was just coincidence that the first three letters seemed pretty good, but we'll try the last one. Y and L gives us T, and our word becomes FIRLT. No, that won't do at all. For a moment I thought we had stumbled on the real secret word, but I guess not." He put down his pencil in exasperation.

"How about 'Baltimore'?" Ted suggested.

"Well, all right, if you're following out a hunch." He calculated for a minute. "That gives us QIQPN. That's much worse than the other."

"Were you telling the truth when you said this table wasn't of much value to you, or did you simply mean that you didn't expect to find the message?"

"What I meant, Ted, was that if the table was destroyed, it wouldn't matter much to me, because I could easily make up a new copy."

"You mean that you've memorized this whole table?" asked Ted incredulously.

"Hardly that, Ted. But I made up the table in the first place. If you were to cut up this table in long strips, and arrange the top alphabet so that it spells out VICTORY, followed by all the remaining letters of the alphabet in order, then you would find the word VICTORY in reverse on each of the lines below. You could then cut the table in the other direction, across the lines, and do the same thing with the alphabet on the side."

"That's very clever." But Ted still remained doubtful. "How do I know that you don't already know the secret word, and are simply holding out on me?"

"Well, I guess there's really no good way to prove it, Ted, any more than I can prove that you didn't fake this message. But perhaps if I told you more about this business, it would convince you.

"My father did not know Mr. Franton before the day he walked into our office, and we never saw or heard from him afterward. In a way, he wasn't even sure that he wanted to consult an attorney. He was reluctant to tell the whole story to us so there didn't seem much we could do for him.

"He had a secret of some sort, but couldn't quite bring himself to divulge it. He wanted his interests protected in case something should happen to him, but was prepared to handle matters for himself if it didn't. As you see, he didn't fully trust lawyers. My father suggested he make out a will, but he didn't think it would be of much use at that time, and the truth is that he appeared to possess very little property—in fact, he seemed darned near broke.

"Another lawyer would have handed him his walking papers, but my father gets intrigued by things like this. I'd been a bug on cryptography, and he suggested that I give Mr. Franton a secret system for writing messages. It happened that I had this table already prepared, so I gave Mr. Franton a copy and told him how to use it. Later he could send us a message written in cipher, but he would retain the secret key word, which he would carry around with him in his wallet. If something should happen to him, there would be no secret message found that could get into the wrong hands, possibly turned over to some expert who could break it. My father would probably be informed about the secret word, following instructions in Mr. Franton's wallet, but if we learned of his death and did not know the secret word, we could turn the message over to an expert ourselves to see what could be done with it. If this all seems unnecessarily complicated to you, it fitted Mr. Franton's personality perfectly. He asked a lot of questions about this cipher system, until he knew how to use it, was satisfied that it was safe enough, and that I could not break it."

"Just how safe is it?" asked Ted.

"If both the table and the key word are kept secret, if messages are short and infrequent, and perhaps the key word changed with later messages, then it would challenge the skill of the best experts. If the table were known but the key word was secret, then it would be easier, but still couldn't be read by just any person who happened along. I told him the truth when I said that I wouldn't be able to break it without the key word, provided he observed the precautions I just mentioned. This seemed to satisfy him.

"Then he walked out of our office, but not out of our lives. He did not write us a message immediately, probably because he didn't have the information he needed, but we expected to receive it shortly. We never did, and would have thought that he had changed his mind about having us represent him, except that he had apparently given our office as a mailing address. One of the things we received was a bill for a large insurance policy, much larger than a man in his circumstances would normally carry, suggesting that perhaps he had been quite affluent at one time. We couldn't reach him, and it seemed a shame to let his policy lapse, so my father paid the premium. That was a year ago, and we've just received the notice for another annual premium. My father is good-hearted, but how long should this thing go on?

"Mr. Franton hadn't told us much, but he did say he had a secret, he mentioned heirs, and he did let slip a reference to Sandy Hill. Of course that didn't help us much, for there are hundreds of Sandy Hills in our country. But a few days ago, when I saw a brief mention of a plane crash on Sandy Hill, I had a hunch about it, flew out here, and picked up the trail of the Frantons. I came out here partly to find any message Mr. Franton might have left, partly for the key word I would need to read it, and partly for any other clues I might pick up. Have I told you enough to convince you that I don't know the secret word? Certainly Mr. Franton wouldn't have given both the message and the key word to me, for then he might as well have told me the whole thing straight out."

"But he didn't give you the message," Ted reasoned. "How do I know that he didn't give you the key word, while with-holding the message?"

"Then the message might have fallen into the wrong hands, while a key word alone would be useless. I have an idea he didn't quite know whether to trust somebody or not. And I think it is obvious that he did intend to send the message to me, and only placed it in the chair temporarily, but the fire came too soon."

"All right, you've convinced me." Ted made a copy of the message, and gave it to Cox. "If you do find the right key word, will you let me know?"

"Yes, if the interests of my client permit. Otherwise, no, obviously. But you might enjoy hunting for it yourself. A key word is usually one that a person would never forget. I talked with Jake Pastor to try and pick up local names and local gossip."

"One more thing," said Ted, as Cox folded up his copy and put it in his pocket, leaving the Vigenère table for Ted, "do you think Mr. Franton's secret had anything to do with oil?"

Cox gave him a shrewd glance. "Yes, it might have been about oil, or about one of a hundred other things I could mention," and he turned and left the room.

CHAPTER 12.

LOST

Oil! The possibility was an exciting one. Suppose there was oil on Sandy Hill. Who was the rightful owner, would he get his rights, or was the whole thing up for grabs? Simply suspecting the presence of oil there was not enough. There would still remain the vast task of organization and financing. The chances were that Jeff Leonard, and whoever he was associated with, had already beaten everyone on the matter of leases; for everyone else it would be too late.

As they had already discussed the possibility of prospecting, Nelson was not particularly surprised by Ted's suggestion of oil.

"If anybody's going to have some good luck, then bully for them. Is that what you and Cox were talking about? I saw you up here, but didn't want to intrude."

Ted told him about the code message and what Cox had said.

"Well, that seems to answer a good many questions, but not the most important ones," Nelson remarked. "He told you what he was doing, but he didn't tell you what he was doing *here*."

Ted was surprised. Thinking back, he realized that Nelson was correct, and this started a new chain of thought for him.

"Nel, there's something we've been missing. Let me mention a few random things and see if they can be put together. I went to Monroe, and read newspaper accounts of two things: Tony's arrival, and the Franton fire. I couldn't find anything else that seemed to relate to this community at all. It's a good rule, when two unusual things happen, to look for a. connection between them, but there doesn't appear to be any connection at all. Then Cox mentioned the possibility of heirs, but he didn't explain why he chose to come to *this* farm. All right, one more thing. We went to the auction this morning, but one thing there seemed very much out of place. What was it? Think about everything that went up for sale."

Nelson ran through the list in his own mind. "You mean that little wagon?"

"Yes. Why a wagon? It was too little to be useful. It was really a toy. Are you with me?"

Nelson whistled. "I'm right there with you, Ted. This is beginning to sound deep, deep, deep. But there are still plenty of things that have to be explained if your theory is going to hold water. If Tony is really the Frantons' little girl, why is it that nobody knew anything about her?"

"I can only offer some possibilities. They were newcomers here, and nobody knew very much about the family. Nobody really had a chance to get acquainted. It's true that Bob rode over to talk with them, and maybe some of the other neighbors did, too, but maybe it just happened that they didn't see the little girl, and no mention was made of her. It's also possible that Mr. Franton was keeping her hidden for some reason, though it's hard to see why. Surely he couldn't have hoped to hide her for very long.

"Another difficulty is that there was a two weeks' lapse between the fire and Tony's arrival here. She was well cared for, and couldn't have been wandering around by herself for that long a time. If that was true, then somebody does know more about Tony than has ever come out. But if anyone else ever suspected Tony was the Frantons' daughter, the idea must have been abandoned, for the two things seemed too far apart.

"We do know, at least, that Cox suspected it, and that is why he chose this farm, and why he took all those pictures of Tony. I've been critical of him before, but if this is what he suspected, I certainly give him credit for keeping the thing quiet until he could check into it. There was no use getting the Fontaines all upset over it, until he was able to prove it."

"Does it really matter who Tony is, Ted? The Fontaines wanted to adopt her anyway, and her real parents are dead."

This was the one point Ted could not talk quite frankly about. "Well, if her identity could be established, it might make things run more smoothly on this adoption business. And Cox did mention a large insurance policy, which would be payable to her, plus the fact that she would be the heir to any other property the Frantons might have possessed."

"What do we do now, Ted?"

"It's hard to know just what we can do. Cox is working on it already, and if we are both working on behalf of Tony, then it would seem that we are allies. One thing I want to do is to check into this oil business a little more so I'll know what I'm talking about. Is there a library around here somewhere?"

"Bob. and I are planning to drive over to Weymouth tomorrow for a new part for the tractor. There might be one there."

"If there is, I'll go along."

When it came time for the three boys to leave in the morning, Tony begged so hard to go with them that the visitors felt sorry for her. Bob and his mother had agreed beforehand that the trip would be too long for her, but though Bob would have relented, his mother did not.

As they drove along, Ted and Nelson were weighed down by the secret they were keeping from Bob, and the restraint this placed on the conversation, but Bob did not seem to notice.

"You should hear Jake Pastor carrying on about his horse," Bob related. "He claims it's the smartest critter ever born. He tells about how he sends her to fetch his pipe, and she walks right up to the window, sticks her head in, and brings the pipe back to him. Funny thing, though, she won't give up the pipe until he lights it and she takes a few puffs first. Then if Jake sees he's got a good audience, he'll go on and tell about his horse jumping rope. He gets on her back and holds the rope in his two hands, and she'll get up on her hind legs and jump as high as a hundred and seventeen. And she blows smoke rings all the while, too!"

"Now I just might be able to believe in a horse learning to fetch a pipe," Nelson decided, "but the jumping rope and the smoke rings make it a little too much. Wouldn't Jake be better off if he toned his stories down a little, so somebody would believe him?"

"Oh, I don't think he cares whether anyone believes him or not."

Arriving at Weymouth, Bob and Nelson went off in search of their equipment, while Ted stopped in at the library, found a book on the subject of oil, and was soon engrossed in this interesting study.

Oil, so the present theory ran, was formed from sea plants and animals which settled to the bottom, became covered with sediment, and slowly decomposed. It was advantageous if the water was stagnant and poisonous at lower levels, for then scavenger fish could not feed upon the bodies. If oil was to be found, it was necessary that the land must at one time have been under the sea. Much of the North American continent was at one time covered by a vast inland sea, and this seemed to include their own locality.

Many other conditions were necessary to the formation of oil. Certain kinds of rocks must be present. Pockets or traps must be formed by the folding of the earth's crust, with a layer of shale or clay above so that the oil cannot escape. Ted also learned about salt plugs. These are pillars of salt, perhaps a mile in diameter, which push up through the rocks. Sometimes a mound of earth above the surface will indicate the presence of a salt plug beneath, which suggests the strong possibility of oil. Was Sandy Hill itself such a mound, sitting upon a salt plug beneath? Ted was beginning to think so, or at least that this was the clue others were following up.

To determine whether oil might be present in a promising location, a test well is often sunk to learn whether the formation of rocks below the surface is such that oil is likely. But short of a test well, there are many other methods. A very delicate balance showing variations in gravity will often disclose the presence of a salt plug. Also, explosions of dynamite are sometimes set off, and by measuring the rate of speed with which the shock waves travel through the earth, salt plugs can be located.

The whole study proved even more complicated than Ted had guessed, and he wished he could follow it up further, but it was time for him to meet the others. He found that they had purchased what they needed, and they kidded all the way home about something which had happened in connection with the purchase, without telling Ted what it was.

But all this laughter vanished when Mrs. Fontaine came out to meet them anxiously.

"Bob, did you take Tony with you after all? She hasn't been seen since you left."

"Of course not, Mom," said Bob, alarmed. "You know I wouldn't do that without telling you."

"I know, but I thought perhaps you had sent her back to tell me, and she only pretended to. We've searched the farm as best we can, but of course there are hundreds of places she might be hiding. She might have lain down in the cornfield and fallen asleep, but it's been so long now, and she's seldom sleepy in the morning. I thought she knew better than to wander off into the woods, but that must be where she went. I didn't want to call in the neighbors until I was sure she was missing."

"You'd better call up and down the line, Mom, and get a search party out. There's no telling how far she's gone by now, and we've got to find her before dark."

Cougar came up to them not very boisterously, and Bob said to him reproachfully, "Where'd she go, boy? I thought she'd be safe as long as she was with you."

The dog slunk along with his tail between his legs, knowing he had been scolded but not understanding the reason why.

Mrs. Fontaine had hurried off toward the house, but Bob started off toward the stables on a trot with Ted and Nelson right behind him. They saw the men in the fields, searching up and down the rows of corn.

"Where could she have wandered off to?" asked Ted.

"I don't think she wandered off," said Bob bitterly. "The hermit's got her, that's what. My father's too generous. We should have done something about him as soon as we found him."

Bob was busy getting Starlight saddled, and Ted said, "I'm coming with you. You may need help."

"What about me?" Nelson requested.

"Two will be enough," said Bob, shaking his head, "and Humpty-Dumpty will hold us back. I'd much rather you stayed here, Nel, and took charge of organizing the searching party until my father gets back. It's possible I'm wrong. She wouldn't deliberately wander off, but something might have attracted her until she got confused about which way was home and kept going in the wrong direction. But I'm betting it's the hermit."

And in a flash of intuition Ted felt that Bob was right. It was the hermit, and had been the hermit all along. He had not merely helped himself when he was hungry, but he had become so familiar around the farm that Cougar had made friends with him. It was the hermit who had visited the wreck and carried something heavy away with him. It was the hermit who had watched Tony playing in the meadow, and this morning had managed to entice her away. Perhaps they had made a mistake in not suggesting a guard for Tony and keeping from the Fontaines the things they knew or suspected about her, but who would have dreamed that she was in danger on the farm with so many people about, and Cougar usually close at her side?

Bob and Ted were ready in a few minutes, and took off up toward the ridge. The drought had continued, and dried-out twigs snapped beneath the horses' hoofs, while a low cloud of dust rose as they passed, even in the woods beneath the trees. This was the most dangerous time of the year, as far as fires were concerned, and the rangers would be particularly alert for any indication of smoke. In fact, as Ted rode, he wondered if he could detect the scent of smoke in the air. The sun was bright in a cloudless sky, rather gray in color like the haze of autumn. That didn't necessarily mean anything; particles of dust often carried for hundreds of miles. Even a fire might not be important, for the rangers sometimes started brush fires themselves to eliminate a possible hazard.

All the time Bob watched the trail before them, but gave no sign that the hermit and Tony had come this way. Either they had taken another trail, or perhaps the hermit, even if he had taken Tony, was not returning to his cabin with her. Maybe the only reason he had ever been up in the gulch was because of Tony, and now that he had secured her he would depart for an unknown destination. Could it be that Tony, who had come so suddenly and so strangely, would disappear in the same fashion?

These thoughts spurred Ted on to keep up with Bob, who was riding as though there wasn't a moment to lose. What had led Tony to go off with this strange man, Ted wondered. He felt sure she had left voluntarily. If there had been any sort of commotion, surely one of the farm workers would have heard it. Nor would it have been a simple matter to bribe her, for she was a little shy with strangers.

Never had Ted imagined that they could reach the gulch in so short a time; yet never had each minute seemed so long. Starlight and Meadowlark appeared to sense the importance of the mission they were on, and rode determinedly.

At the mouth of Rainbow Gulch, Bob gave a startled cry and leaped from his horse. Some short distance off the trail the soil had been recently dug up and replaced, leaving a little mound.

"I didn't notice that before," Ted observed.

"It wasn't there. Ride!" and Bob was back in the saddle, and turning up the gulch followed by Ted.

They rode under the Rainbow and farther up the gulch through its many turnings, their pace necessarily slowed. But now the horses became a problem. It was clear that they did not want to go up the gulch. It took Ted's utmost urging to keep Meadowlark moving ahead, and she made it very clear that if given free rein she would turn about and head for home. Again Ted thought he could smell smoke, and decided that the hermit must have his fire going again, though the day was warm. This was no doubt what the horses had sensed and interpreted as a menace.

If the hermit had a rifle—and there was a good chance he did—he might be lying in wait for anyone who was pursuing because he had taken Tony. It was a dangerous thing to come charging up the gulch. It would have been better to take time out to circle around and come upon him unawares. But Bob, rushing to Tony's rescue, had thrown all prudence to the winds, nor would Ted urge caution upon him. Besides, he could not think of the hermit as a cunning, ruthless man, a prospector determined to get what he wanted at all costs. Instead, he saw him as a sick, confused old man, who sometimes hung about the farm, looking for food and longing for companionship; a man who muttered to himself over strange things that no one else could understand; who had caught a glimpse of Tony and taken a queer fancy to her, seeing no reason why he shouldn't take her away with him if he wished.

The next turn would bring them within sight of the cabin, Ted thought. Just then he lost control of his horse and Meadowlark tossed him before she turned and bolted back down the gulch. Bob drew rein.

"Are you hurt, Ted?" he asked in annoyance, as though afraid that Ted would delay him.

"No, go ahead. I'll follow on foot."

As Ted rounded the turn at a jog, the source of the little stream came into sight, then the path down which they had crept on their first visit, then the cabin itself. There was a strange stillness in the air. No birds were to be heard, and Ted recalled that all signs of life had been missing all through the woods. No rabbits had scurried across the path or chipmunks run chattering up the trees. There in the little clearing before the cabin all was quiet; a chance passer-by would have thought it was deserted. The bubbling of the spring and the clatter of Starlight's hoofs were the only sounds to be heard.

Ted saw Bob make his last dash across the clearing, where he drew up and was off Starlight's back almost before she stopped, then threw the reins over her head. He sprinted toward the cabin and threw his shoulder against the door, expecting it to be locked, but it gave easily at his touch and he tumbled inside.

CHAPTER 13.

A REMARKABLE RECOVERY

When Ted pushed into the cabin, he saw with relief that Tony was there, and apparently unharmed. She was sitting in the chair, poised and not at all frightened. Across from her sat the hermit, a stooped old man with flowing white beard and a puzzled expression on his face, as though pondering on things which were too difficult to figure out.

Tony, who had been speaking to Bob, looked up as Ted entered, and said very casually, "Hello, Ted."

"Tony! We've been looking all over for you."

"I came to talk with this man. He said if I'd come he'd tell me my name."

"He did?" Bob exclaimed. "What is your name?"

"He hasn't told me yet."

Ted turned to the old man. He hadn't seemed to resent their arrival; instead it was just another part of the puzzle he was trying to understand.

"What is her name, sir?" asked Ted gently.

The hermit did not answer, and Tony said in her best grown-up manner, "You mustn't get him excited. He's trying to think of it."

They could not tell whether the hermit really knew her correct name; he might have used the offer to tell her as a pretext to lure her away. But then, how had he known there was any mystery about her name?

Though they would have liked to take Tony away as soon as they could, they found they couldn't leave immediately. Much as Bob wanted to carry the good news to his mother and father and the others, he realized the old man was in need of help. He wasn't a queer old prospector guarding a claim, as they had thought. He was someone badly needing assistance.

"Have you been here long, sir?" asked Bob.

The hermit considered the question for some moments before replying, "A long time."

"What is your name, sir, and what are you doing here?"

This time the hermit did not attempt to reply, and they could not tell whether he had really forgotten his name, or whether the matter of his identity was so repulsive he could not answer.

Ted looked about the cabin. There were a few cans of food, though the stock was pitifully small, but it indicated at least that someone had been taking care of the hermit. But the flour barrel proved to be empty, coffee and sugar were low, and there were only a few matches. Whoever had been supplying the hermit hadn't been taking very good care of him lately. That would account for the missing sheep.

The cabin itself, though rudely furnished, seemed to be as neatly kept as the hermit was capable of in his condition, and the hermit himself, though his clothes were rough, had obviously made an effort to keep up his appearance. His hair was brushed, his hands and shirt clean—and on his feet was a pair of half-boots with the odd-shaped toe.

Still alert enough to catch their studying glances, the hermit asked tremulously, "Did you bring a razor? They wouldn't ever bring me a razor."

"I'm sorry, sir," Bob responded, "that I don't have a razor. Who was it that wouldn't bring you a razor?"

"*They* wouldn't," said the hermit impatiently, as though that explained everything.

"Was it the man in the plane? Did you know the man in the plane? Did you see it crash?" Ted asked.

This was altogether too confusing for the hermit. The look of bewilderment on his face grew, and he shook his head savagely, as though trying to clear his memory.

"The plane crashed," was all he said.

"I know it crashed," said Bob patiently. "Did you see it crash?"

"It crashed in the tree," said the old man.

It was becoming apparent that they weren't going to elicit much useful information from the hermit. It seemed such an effort for him to try to think that Bob didn't have the heart to badger him. He gave up the attempt and turned his attention to Tony.

"Tony, you know you shouldn't have left the farm without telling someone you were going. How did you happen to go away with a strange man?"

"He was kind to me," she answered.

Anyone else who had seen the hermit would have noticed his white beard, stooped posture, and unpressed clothes, but to Tony he had been merely a kind man. Perhaps she had been able to see something in him that no one else could see. Perhaps he *was* a kind man, and that was all that was really important.

"What about Cougar? Didn't he bark when the hermit came?"

"No, the man patted him and he wagged his tail. That's how I knew it was all right."

This confirmed Ted's suspicions that the hermit had often been around the farm. Perhaps Cougar, too, had judged him on something more than his appearance. He could have been right for the hermit hadn't tried to hurt Tony. Actually, it looked as if he was trying to clear up some of his fogged memories.

"Well, didn't Cougar try to come with you when you left?" Bob went on.

"Yes, but I made him go back. The man said we couldn't take him."

That, at least, cleared Cougar of blame for not staying with Tony. He had been taught to obey members of the family, so that was what he had to do, no matter how badly he wanted to go along. There was no use scolding Tony; her mother would talk to her about it when she returned home.

"What do you think we'd better do, Ted?" asked Bob in a low voice. "I'd like to get back and tell them—goodness knows what they're going to think when Meadowlark shows up—but it's too late to call off the search. Anyway there's only one horse for the four of us."

"Why don't you take Tony home on Starlight, and I'll stay here with the hermit until somebody comes? They're probably on the way already, for Nelson knows where we are."

"I hate to do that, Ted. Starlight needs cooling off, the hermit needs help, and you're my guest."

"A pretty stupid guest to let my horse get away from me."

"Don't give it another thought. It might have happened to me, too, on Meadowlark. Starlight's special. How can I blame you when I took the best horse? Why don't we have something to eat and wait for the others?"

When she was asked, Tony admitted that she had had nothing to eat since breakfast, and so she was hungry. The hermit, too, must be hungry, although the puzzles in his mind were claiming most of his attention.

While Bob built a fire, Ted went through the food supplies available and selected whatever he could use.

When their lunch was ready, Tony drew her chair up to the table, and the hermit joined them with only a little persuasion. He ate, but in a mechanical fashion, as if he hardly knew what he was eating. His eyes remained fastened upon Tony most of the time, as though somehow she could help him, but he said nothing.

As they were eating, Starlight nickered several times from outside, and Tony asked, "Why is she making so much noise?"

"Oh, I suppose she wants to start for home. I've tied her so she won't wander off."

Starlight's whinnying continued at intervals, becoming ever more insistent, until Bob went outside to see what the trouble was. As Ted followed him out the door, the smell of smoke became more pronounced. He remembered now that the odor had been strong as they rode up the gulch, though there had been no fire in the cabin when they arrived.

It was the smoke that was alarming Starlight. Her nostrils were quivering, and pointed directly toward the source, a cloud of wisps rising from beyond the gulch.

Tony had also run outside, and noticed the smoke. "Where is all the smoke coming from, Bob?"

"Oh, there must be a little brush fire somewhere," he answered, trying to make his voice sound casual. "We'd better think about starting for home."

"That's no brush fire,' said a firm voice behind him. "It's a real forest fire, and we're already cut off from the mouth of the gulch."

They turned to see the hermit standing in the doorway of the cabin. It was the same man they had seen before, and yet he seemed different. He was standing perfectly erect, so that it could be seen that he was a tall man—taller than either of the boys—and of firm build. His voice no longer whined, his face had lost its bewildered look, his eyes were resolute and purposeful.

"We can't be cut off," said Bob desperately. "A fire couldn't spread that fast."

"It doesn't take much of a wind to spread it when everything's this dry, once it has a good start. And this one looks like it has a good start, all right. There won't be much of these woods left after today."

"But maybe it's not past the gulch. Maybe we can still get out," said Bob anxiously, watching the layers of smoke rising slowly into view.

Ted stood by, awaiting the decision of the others who knew more about these things than he did.

"No, it's too late for that," said the hermit firmly, and though Bob seemed less certain of his directions down the winding gulch, he showed that this was probably right.

"But we can't just wait here, sir," Bob argued. "The fire may creep up the gulch. It may be able to make the turns. Even if it doesn't, it may start sweeping down the hills. There must be a way out of here."

"There's a way out, I think, for a man on horseback, but it's too late to make it on foot. A rider could climb the hill and circle around through the other gulches."

One horse—and four people. There wasn't any way they could all ride to safety. Any attempt to overload Starlight would lessen her chance of getting through, and might lose everything for them.

"Suppose a rider could get through, what could he do?"

The hermit shook his head slowly. "I don't know, but maybe the rangers will be able to fight their way back with a rescue party. It seems the only chance."

"Then if someone has to ride for help, I'll go," Bob volunteered. "Starlight is used to me, and I'd have the best chance."

"Do you know which paths to take, which ones the horse can climb?"

"No, but—"

"Then you'll never find them in time. I'll be the one to go," said the hermit with quiet logic.

And they knew he was right. But if the boys couldn't get out, wasn't there at least a chance for Tony? The responsibility was Bob's to decide what was best for her.

"Well, look, sir, if you think you can make it, take Tony with you."

"Tony? The little girl? Her name's Marilyn. She may be glad to know it someday."

He looked down fondly at the little girl, and no one could mistake the pure devotion in his eyes.

"Then take her," Bob urged, but the hermit shook his head.

"No, I'm not that sure."

Then the danger was worse than the hermit had hinted. He knew the course he must take, and how slim was his chance of getting through. Now Bob and Ted knew it, too.

Starlight had been pawing the ground nervously, and Bob attempted to soothe her with a few whispered words.

"Easy there, big girl. There's a lot depending on you. You've got to get through. You've got to run like you've never run before."

She flicked her ears as though she understood, and wanted to assure them that every muscle in her powerful body would be straining to do what he had asked of her.

"Stay by the stream as long as you can," advised the hermit in a low voice. "You'll be easier to find. But if you see you're in danger of getting trapped here, go straight east. That will be the safest place for the next few hours. Stay off the plateau to the west. The fire will race across the grass once it reaches there."

He patted Tony on the head, sprang upon Starlight's back and they were off down the gulch. As the pair disappeared about the turn, the boys had only a moment to marvel at the miracle that had brought the hermit to his senses in their hour of need, before turning to their own danger.

Tony tugged at Bob's sleeve. "Is Marilyn really my name, Bob?"

"I don't know, Tony. Maybe it is."

She seemed to be saying it over and over to herself. "I hope it is. That's a pretty name. It doesn't sound at all like a boy's name, does it, Ted?"

"No, it's not a boy's name," he agreed.

They were busy watching the columns of smoke announce the advance of the forest fire upon them. There seemed no question but that it was now closer and heavier. To the east, where the hermit must ride, the black clouds were threatening, and they knew he was going to have tough going. To the west, over the plateau above the gulch, the sky seemed lighter, but this was the opposite direction from that the hermit had advised them to take.

"Where did that man go?" Tony questioned.

"Oh, he went to tell the rangers about the fire," Ted answered.

"Well, when is he coming back?"

"I don't think he's coming back, Tony. He'll send the rangers back, and then we'll help them fight the forest fire. Won't that be fun?"

Somewhat dubiously, Tony agreed that it might be fun, but there was a further question in her mind. "Is this fire like the other one?"

"What other one, Tony? What do you mean?"

But the gossamer thread of memory was too fragile, and she was unable to answer.

Bob spoke to Ted in a soft voice. "The fire's advancing up the gulch. I think it's still two turns away. I don't know whether it can make the turns. If it makes the second-to-last one, we'll have to be ready, and if it makes the last one we'll go."

"All right, Bob, whatever you say."

"Awfully sorry I got you into this, Ted. I had to look for Tony, of course, but there was no reason to drag you into it."

"You didn't drag me into anything. I came because I wanted to."

"Anyway, thanks. And you're doing the right thing with Tony. Let's make her think it's a game, just as long as we can."

To the east the clouds of smoke were closing in. No one could have gotten through on foot, and even a man on horseback would be unable to make it now. Whether the hermit and Starlight had been able to get through before the fire closed in was uncertain, but all they could do was to hope fervently that they had. But even if they did, it was too late for the rangers to fight their way back along the same path. They would have to come another way.

Tony was watching the advancing smoke with interest. She didn't appear to be frightened, but they knew that she was taking her cue from them. As long as they didn't seem alarmed, she wouldn't be frightened either. This thought steadied them down for the job they had to do, and they did their best to appear matter-of-fact and unconcerned.

"This is a big fire, isn't it, Ted?" asked Tony with wide eyes.

"Yes, pretty big, but not as big as some of them."

"Will all the big trees get burned up?"

"I'm afraid so, Tony, most of them."

"Will the rabbits get burned up, too?" she asked with deep concern.

"No, I don't think so. I believe the rabbits can tell when the fire is coming, and they run away before it gets to them."

"But don't their houses get burned up?"

"Oh, that doesn't matter very much to rabbits. They just start new homes somewhere else."

"Oh." She seemed satisfied that the rabbits were safe, and so this principle worry was off her mind, never dreaming that their own situation was more critical than the rabbits'.

"Will the rangers bring a fire engine with them?"

"Hm, no, I don't think so. I guess a fire engine isn't of much use in fighting a fire like this."

It appeared that the fire had made the second-to-last turn successfully. The rising columns of smoke were even closer, and Bob no longer had confidence that the final turn could halt the steady advance. Even among the rocky ledges trees and bushes were too numerous. They must get ready to leave.

CHAPTER 14.

TONY'S GAME

Reluctant though the boys were to leave the little stream, they knew it wasn't wide enough to offer them much protection from the flames advancing up the gulch. Even should they crouch in the middle of the stream, the heat from the fire and the heavy smoke overhead would be too much for them. Yet they knew that once the smoke came close to them, they would feel a pressing need for water.

They went into the cabin in search of a container for water. But search though they would, the cabin offered nothing in the way of a closed container that they could carry with them. The next best thing was rags which could be soaked in water. The found a number of these and took them back to the stream.

Bob could see the danger was coming closer from another direction. Even faster than the advance of the flames up the gulch was their march along the crest of the hill to the west. It was apparent to Bob that if they waited much longer, they stood a chance of being cut off from that direction and hopelessly trapped in the gulch. He explained matters in a low voice to Ted.

"That hill where we came down the other day is our only chance for getting out of here with Tony. If the fire reaches the top, we're out of luck."

"Then let's go." Ted was decisive, in the absence of an alternative.

They soaked the rags in the stream until they had absorbed as much moisture as they could hold. Then Bob made them up into a knapsack which he strapped to Ted's back.

"Tony," he said casually, "I guess it's about time for us to leave."

"Where are we going? Are we going home?"

"No, not just yet. We're going up the hill and see how the fire's coming, so we can tell the rangers when they get here. You'd better take a good long drink first."

"I'm not thirsty, Bob."

"Take a drink anyway. We may not be near any water for a while, so it'll have to last."

Under his urging she drank as much as she could. Then the boys drank, too, and splashed water on their faces and hair. Without being told, Tony did the same.

"All right, Tony, let's go."

"If my name's Marilyn, when are you going to start calling me that?"

"I don't know, Tony," Bob responded. "We'll figure that out after the fire's over."

Though the three boys had climbed up this hill quite easily when they were alone, it wasn't going to be easy with Tony clinging to them. Bob had thought of taking Tony on his back and creeping up on hands, feet, and knees, but Ted thought it would be better if they each took one of her hands. In this manner they began the climb. They soon discovered another factor which made this climb more difficult. The other day they had worn outdoor shoes which gave better traction. The dress shoes the boys had worn to town were slippery on the soles, and the ground seemed to be sliding beneath their feet.

They would have made poor progress on their feet alone. But they looked for shrubs, tufts of grass, and roots of trees to cling to, and in this way they inched their way slowly upward. And yet, with victory almost in sight, they came near to failure after all. The top of the hill was a sandy bank without rocks or vegetation of any kind. The previous time the boys had given each other a little boost and a helping hand over this obstacle, and made it without difficulty. But today the situation was different.

Tony's feet began to slip, and she had no free hands to help herself. Bob, in trying to help her, lost his balance as well. If they all went sprawling, they were due for a nasty tumble, perhaps all the way down to the foot of the hill. How much more time did they have to reach the top of the hill, how many more attempts could they make before their strength gave out? Tony was a lovable but heavy lodestone upon them. Even she had sensed something of the tenseness of the moment, and without saying a word was holding as still as possible, so as not to jiggle Bob further.

Fortunately Ted had a firmer footing. His free right hand dug in the dirt, and to his great surprise and relief, he found a tree root, completely hidden but only lightly covered with dirt. With this to help him, he kept his balance until the others had recovered, and then they scrambled up the rest of the way. Coming so soon after the hermit's recovery, they could only look upon it as another miracle, something to be accepted without being understood.

They stood up and brushed the dirt off their clothes. For the first time the flames themselves were now within view—closer than the boys had hoped—and Tony gave a gasp of surprise. She looked from one to the other. Bob was watching the fire with close interest, and didn't look at all concerned, so she decided that everything must be all right.

"That was a pretty big hill, wasn't it?" she remarked.

"Oh, pretty big," Ted answered casually, "but there are some a lot bigger."

They still were not certain how pressing their danger was. A little rise lay some distance ahead of that. From there they would be able to see the whole plateau, and could gain a much better idea of their situation. Slowly the trio made their way upward to the edge of the plateau.

It was Bob's responsibility to keep their bearings clearly in mind, for Ted was much less certain about directions and the lay of the land. Bob tried his best to explain matters to him.

"It's sweeping in from the southwest. Across this plateau to the west, there's that trail leading down and across to Sandy Hill. There's no closer passage down the steep cliffs stretching across to the north. And to the east are those series of gulches, with their heavily wooded ridges, which we will have to cross to get back to the valley and its farms. That's the way the hermit went—and got through, we hope."

Far across the plateau a finger of flame was racing, threatening to cut off their only escape by way of Sandy Hill.

"Do we run for it?" asked Ted quietly.

"That's the panic road, Ted, and it means disaster. We'd be running into the fire instead of away from it, and fire travels fast through this dry grassland. The hermit was right. This plateau is no place for us. We'll have to circle back around the head of the gulch until we're on the eastern side—away from the grass and back to the trees—but always with those impassable cliffs at our backs. I was hoping one of the rangers' planes could land on the plateau and take us off, but it can't be done. One of those small planes might crash-land here, but it could never take off again."

"What about a helicopter?"

"I haven't seen a helicopter around here since a year or two back, and with the smoke cover closing in it will soon be difficult to find us, even if it does get here."

But this was said in such a way that Tony could hear little and understand less.

"Come on, Tony, we're going this way," Bob urged her cheerfully, turning her away from the walls of flame advancing in their steady, irresistible march. He glanced anxiously upward toward a burning sun amid a cloudless sky, and Ted, too, followed his example, searching for some sign of a plane—of any plane. But there was none in sight; it was too early to expect them.

From that moment a feeling, not of panic, but of quiet despair settled over the boys. But they were determined they must try to keep Tony from being frightened for as long as they could.

"I'm glad it was the hermit, instead of me, who rode for help," Bob mused. "I hope Starlight's going to be all right."

And Ted understood perfectly: if it came to a choice between safety for himself or danger with Tony, Bob preferred the latter. Somehow Ted felt that he did, too, and his sympathy went out to Nelson, helplessly fuming on the other side of that barrier of flames.

The boys were surprised by their own coolness. They could look upon the advancing flames almost with detachment. The fire seemed to reach from the rocky uplands at one end in a huge crescent to the valley below the cliffs at the other, and they themselves were inside the crescent. Here and there long fingers crept out in advance, like the one they had last seen on the plateau. Later the main line of conflagration would advance and fill out the pockets, reducing trees and grass alike to a charred waste. The grass would recover first, however, and within a year or two there would be little sign of the fire which had swept through. But the forest of Bob's boyhood would be nothing more than a memory.

The crackling of the fire was becoming audible to them for the first time as the hungry flames advanced relentlessly, with an insatiable appetite. There would be a sudden puff of smoke up into the air as another tree was caught in the advance. Then, for a few minutes it would appear that the greedy flames were satisfied, until another tree ahead would go up with a mighty puff of smoke. And in this manner, a few feet at a time, the flames leaped steadily toward them. The wind, however, was blowing the smoke out ahead of the fire, so that the thick cloud was almost overhead. Their throats were beginning to get a little parched, though fortunately the damp rags helped out until they were dry and Bob discarded them. Pretty soon Tony would realize she was thirsty, and would begin to beg for water, a moment they dreaded.

She could not avoid watching the fire with wide, fascinated eyes. It was something new, of course, but she accepted it without realizing the dangers it held for them. The boys neither encouraged her to look at the fire, nor told her to look away. Meanwhile, without seeming to be in retreat, Bob was slowly leading them away around the end of the gulch to the safer area directly east. The fire moved rather slowly through the forest, but at the edge of the plateau, the fingers of flame would begin racing, like a team of sprinters in a mad dash through the dry grass to the cliffs.

"When will the rangers come?" asked Tony, not quite fearful as yet, but as though seeking reassurance that everything was all right.

"Pretty soon, I hope, Tony."

"Why don't we pretend we're rangers, too, and help them put out the fire?" Ted suggested.

"How will they put out the fire?" she asked, for young as she was she could see that this fire, with flames shooting high into the air, was a big job for a whole army of rangers.

"Oh, they have different ways, don't they, Bob?"

"Yes," he answered absently. "Sometimes they set off a big explosion. Sometimes they start another fire in front of this one, so that the two fires sort of fight each other, and put each other out. And sometimes they plow up a long strip of land so that the fire can't get across."

"Is that what they'll do here, Bob?" she asked hopefully.

"I don't know. We'll have to wait and see."

Though Bob was glad that he could offer hope of safety, his glance at Ted indicated that he didn't believe any of these things would be successful. The fire was moving steadily ahead; the unburned area along the rim of the forest was growing smaller. They didn't know how much longer they had, but it was probably an hour or two at most.

It seemed to Ted also that the rangers were going to have little success in stopping this fire anywhere along the line. This particular section would burn itself out at the cliffs, but along the valley at one end, and past the plateau and on toward Sandy Hill at the other, the fire would race until it reached the next firebreak. There, with good luck and the absence of a high wind, it would be halted. Fortunately, the farms were probably safe, and he was thankful for that.

Tony continued to watch the black smoke and the roaring flames.

"How are the rangers going to get here, Bob?" she demanded.

"I couldn't say, Tony. They'll come whichever is the best way. That's something for them to figure out."

"Well, I wish they'd get here soon so we could begin to play the game."

"Why don't we begin the game right now, Tony?" Ted proposed. "We'll pretend we're scouts, and we have to watch how the fire's going so we can report to the rangers, and they'll know how to fight it."

"It's going this way," she said with a shaky voice.

"Yes, part of it's coming this way, but part of it's going another way. Over there, past the plateau, it's burning the other way. We'll have to remember all that so we can tell the rangers."

It was clear now that the plateau would be the first to be overrun with flames. Fortunately they were now to the east of the gulch, which was probably the safest place in the woods, if anything on the windward side of the fire could be said to be safe. It gave them a little more time, and the trees cut off their view of the plateau, so that Tony did not see what the boys knew was now happening. The fire must have reached the edge of the grassland all along the line, and the plateau would be burned over within a few minutes.

"If we're scouts," said Tony, "are we supposed to report everything we see?"

"That's right," Ted assured her, "everything that has anything to do with the fire."

"If we saw an airplane, are we supposed to report that?"

"I think we should." He was startled. "Where do you see an airplane?"

"Over there." She pointed with her finger through the trees.

The smoke was heavy, but in a moment the plane had emerged, and the boys were able to spot it. It was one of the rangers' scouting planes. They felt slightly relieved. It was nice to know that the rangers had spotted the fire so soon and were out in force, even if there wasn't much they could do.

"There's another one," Bob said, as another plane came into view from over the valley. "Those are rangers. They're scouting the fire."

"If they're scouting from up there, do we have to scout, too? Can't they see better than we can?"

"Not always, Tony. They can see farther, but they're too high and too far away to see everything. They'll scout the fire from the air, and we'll scout from the ground."

A third plane also appeared, and soon it seemed that they were flying one after the other in a large circle, with the cabin in the gulch as the center. That could mean only one thing: the planes were looking for them. But presently, not finding them, the planes began to move over to the west, apparently believing that it was likely they had gone off in that direction. The boys watched despairingly.

But suddenly there was a shift, and the planes came back to the opposite side of the gulch. To the boys it meant that the hermit had gotten through with his message.

"That means Starlight must have made it," Bob murmured. "Good girl!"

Though the planes were now circling directly overhead, it was not certain that they were going to find them. The haze from the smoke was too heavy, and the occasional trees obscured the view. Unless they were spotted soon, the pilots would probably shift northward to the unburned but heavily wooded section, where Bob had not wanted to take them except as a last resort. If there were only some way they could let the planes know where they were; if it were only possible to amplify their voices, so that they could shout, "Look! We're down here!" and a pilot could hear them.

"A signal—that's what we need," said Bob, patting his pockets.

Not a smoke signal, surely. There was already so much smoke that it would go unnoticed. "Got anything shiny?" asked Ted.

All this time Tony had carried her purse in a strap about her neck. Bob noticed it now, and asked, "What have you got in there, Tony?"

"My dolly's things."

"Open it up and let me see."

She unfastened the clasp, and took out objects one by one. Among the articles she produced was the doll's mirror Nelson had given her.

"I think that will do, Tony. Let me try it."

Bob managed to hold the mirror in such a way that it caught the rays of the sun, then attempted to reflect them back through the trees upon one of the planes. He was almost successful the first time, the rays catching the body of the plane amidship, but the plane continued on its way into the haze. He then concentrated on the plane which followed, aiming at the nose of the plane, trying to get the rays in the pilot's eyes. He must have succeeded, for a moment later the pilot swung out of line and the plane began to arch over in their direction.

Tony asked with a tremor in her voice, "Are the planes going to land now?"

"We don't know yet, Tony," Ted answered. "Watch, and we'll see." But he knew that these planes couldn't land. A helicopter might do it, but Bob had said he was pretty sure the rangers didn't have a helicopter at this station, and even a helicopter would have trouble among the trees. But Tony was looking more cheerful. The rangers had come. Wouldn't they soon be going home?

"This is an awfully long game, isn't it, Bob? When is it going to be over?"

"Pretty soon, I hope, Tony," he answered, his voice suddenly dull and hopeless. The rangers had found them; they were now so close and still so far away.

The only hope Ted could see was that the rangers drop a large body of fire fighters in by parachute and attempt to block the progress of the fire. But he knew in his heart that all such efforts would be futile. And he knew that it wasn't fair to expect the rangers—for all their bravery—to drop dozens of men into such a dangerous area on the slight chance of rescuing three.

The plane had definitely sighted them. It was flying as low as was safe, in a large circle about them, occasionally dipping its wings as though to encourage them. The other planes had left, apparently to scout the fire farther up the line. The haze was growing heavier, and it would be hard to keep them in view. Holding Tony's hands, they began to walk slowly toward the edge of the gulch, hoping to get a little clear of the trees, though some continued up to the very rim.

The plane was keeping them carefully in sight, with the help of occasional flashes from Bob's signal mirror, adapting its circle to their slow progress. It was on the farthest side of its arc, away from the fire and across the gulch, when suddenly a black speck was seen to leave the plane. Moments later a huge, white, billowing nylon shot out and caught the breeze, and began drifting slowly down.

CHAPTER 15.

ANOTHER FIRE

After Bob and Ted had departed, Nelson returned to the house. Mrs. Fontaine had started the party line on its neighborly work, and then Nelson took over, answering a number of calls that came in. He learned that not a man or older boy anywhere in the district had refused the summons, regardless of the pressure of his own work. How many eventually came Nelson never knew—somewhere between one and two hundred—for they were never assembled in one group.

Some of the neighbor women arrived to stay with Mrs. Fontaine, and then Nelson took off to join the searching parties. It was because of this search that the fire was discovered earlier than might otherwise have happened, even before the forest rangers themselves had spotted it. An alarm was turned in, and an expert team of fire fighters was dispatched to the scene. Even so, the fire had already had a good start.

Discovery of the fire made an immediate difference in the plans for the search. It was decided the best thing was to advance to the fire and see what they could do about combating it. If in this way they happened to pass Tony by, well and good, they could find her later; but if by chance she was already on the other side of the flames— well, that was something they didn't like to think about.

"She must be all right, Rob," one of the men remarked to Mr. Fontaine, when he had been located and finally arrived at the scene. "She couldn't have wandered off this far."

Certainly the fire was quite some distance from the farm, and Mr. Fontaine seemed reassured. He had no reason to doubt that Tony had merely wandered off, for he knew of nothing to connect the hermit with her.

Earlier, Nelson had informed one of the rangers of the possibility that Tony was at the cabin in the gulch, and he had transmitted this information to the searching planes. Should he give the same information to Mr. Fontaine? He was at the point of doing so several times, but something always seemed to intervene, so he kept putting it off. There didn't seem to be much to be gained.

But Mr. Fontaine remembered the hermit, and mentioned him.

"Poor devil!" said one of the farmers. "If he's trapped up there at Rainbow Gulch, I'm afraid it's too late to save him."

"Maybe he isn't there," argued another. "He might have left before this."

"I don't know," said Mr. Fontaine. "The boys said he looked as though he'd been holed up there for a long time."

Barring a sudden shift in wind, it appeared that the farms were safe. This was good news for Mr. Kirstead, whose farm lay close to the woods, with the Fontaine farm just beyond. The other farms should be protected by the road. With the arrival of the ranger fighting unit, efforts became better organized, and the men did what they could to beat back the flames. Jake Pastor, having come out in someone's car, was among the fighters, in deadly earnest and telling no stories now.

Although a protective strip was being plowed up to contain them, the flames showed little tendency to cut back toward the farms. It was on the other side, where the wind was fanning the flames and sending them racing toward the plateau, that the real danger lay. About this the rangers could do nothing.

Where were Bob and Ted? This was the worry that weighed on Nelson's mind. Had they got through to the hermit and was Tony there? If everything had gone smoothly they might have gotten out of the danger area before they were trapped. Perhaps they were safe even now, having come back by another route.

When the newly arrived ranger group heard about the hermit, they shook their heads dubiously. They hoped he wasn't trapped up in the gulch, but if he was there didn't seem any hope of reaching him. The flames were altogether too heavy and the smoke too thick to allow hope that a rescue party could break through.

The leader of the fighting group had hardly finished this pessimistic review when a shout went up from the men. The smoke seemed to open, and a man on horseback was seen to emerge from the burning woods. Mr. Fontaine didn't recognize the rider, but he would have recognized the horse half a mile off.

"Starlight!" he exclaimed, and then a chill seemed to go through him.

As though guided by some instinct—or perhaps it was Starlight's instinct—the rider advanced directly toward Mr. Fontaine. He had made it through the fire, but not without marks. His tangled white beard hung awry, and his face was smudged with black. His shirt had been singed, and the burns beneath must have been painful. Starlight was sweated and nervous, but seemed otherwise uninjured. She drew up in front of Mr. Fontaine with a shiver and a shaking neigh, and the rider slipped to the ground.

"This is Bob's horse," exclaimed Mr. Fontaine, grasping the bridle. "Where is he? What have you done with him?"

The hermit leaned against the saddle for support. "The boys . . . and the little girl . . ." he was breathless and gasping, and had to stop to gather strength to continue. "They're at Rainbow Gulch, near the head. They'll stay there as long as they can, then head directly eastward. I had . . . to get through to tell you. . . ."

The ranger lieutenant—the one whom Nelson had talked to earlier—was close to Mr. Fontaine's side, and the other men gathered around. At the hermit's words a hush spread over the group. Rainbow Gulch—they had all heard it correctly—and someone who ought to know had just said there was no way to reach Tony, Bob, and Ted.

Mr. Fontaine straightened up. As well as any of them he was aware of the great danger which threatened the three. But the least he could do was to show as much courage, faith, and dignity as possible. He turned to the hermit.

"I'm afraid you're not well, sir. I'll drive you in to the hospital."

"The others . . ." the hermit gasped.

"Everything that can be done for them will be done," said Mr. Fontaine quietly, "and I have an obligation to the man who tried to save them."

He turned back toward the lieutenant. "Is there any hope for them?"

"Oh, there's a good chance," the lieutenant responded. "We've got a helicopter on the way. If we're able to find them, we'll pick them up."

"Then you'll let me know at the hospital?"

"The very first chance I get."

"I'll drive you, Mr. Fontaine," Nelson offered. If Mr. Fontaine had been generous, so could he, and the farmer might need help with the injured hermit. Besides, Nelson could not avoid feeling that perhaps he should not have hidden things from Mr. Fontaine, even with the best of intentions.

The lieutenant barked out his orders.

"Contact the planes on the mobile unit and tell them what the man said about looking to the east of the gulch." The man he indicated was off on the run.

But as Mr. Fontaine helped the hermit into the car, the lieutenant shook his head slightly. "Poor guy," Nelson heard him mutter, "I didn't have the heart to tell him the helicopter is still almost two hours away."

On the long drive to the city, the hermit had nothing to say. He seemed to be exhausted, and Mr. Fontaine did not press him, while Nelson tended strictly to the driving. Yet Nelson felt that matters had reached a climax, and that soon they would know all about Tony— the things that had happened leading up to her arrival at the Fontaine farm, what had taken her off with the hermit to Rainbow Gulch, and the explanation of all the other strange events.

At the hospital the hermit was admitted to the receiving room, and Mr. Fontaine was told it might be an hour before he could see him. So they paced the corridors, and put through two calls to the Valley Junction exchange, but there was no news.

The nurse had just told them that they might see the hermit when suddenly Mrs. Manners rushed into the hall, her hair streaming wildly.

"Where is he?" she exclaimed.

"Where is who, Mrs. Manners?"

"That man, that hermit—who was living up at Rainbow Gulch."

"This is his room, but please—"

She brushed past Mr. Fontaine and Nelson and into the room. The hermit, though lying very quiet, turned his head as she entered.

"Where is my husband, Mr. Franton? You've got to tell me.

The hermit answered in a weak voice, "Are you Mrs. Manners? I'm sorry but your husband is dead. He was badly injured in the airplane crash. I found him in the wreck and carried him away to my cabin. I did the best I could to take care of him, brought him fresh meat and milk, but his injuries were too serious. He died, and I buried him at the mouth of the gulch."

Mrs. Manners broke out into sobs, but as Mr. Fontaine tried to comfort her, she said, "It's all right. I suppose I knew he was dead, when I didn't hear from him after the airplane crash. It was just the shock of knowing for sure—"

The raised voices had attracted a nurse, who brought a doctor into the room.

"I'm sorry," said the doctor, "but you people will have to leave. The patient is becoming too excited."

Mr. Fontaine took Mrs. Manners' arm and led her from the room, but turned a moment to speak to the doctor.

"Do you think he will be all right, doctor?"

The doctor shook his head slowly. "The burns, though serious, are only one thing. There seems to be something else. I'm very sorry, but I can't promise you anything at all."

Out on a bench in the corridor, Mrs. Manners had partially regained her self-control.

"I want to tell you all about it," she said, as Mr. Fontaine seated himself at her side, and motioned to Nelson to stay. "With my husband dead there's no longer any reason that I shouldn't, and it will relieve a heavy burden on my conscience."

And so, between renewed sobs, and many repetitions and broken sentences, Mrs. Manners told her strange tale.

Mr. Manners had come from a rather poor family, but his parents had struggled to give him every advantage that they could. By dint of hard scraping, they had managed to provide him with a good education. Going to an exclusive school where all the other boys came from wealthy families only served to arouse his resentment. He became very jealous that other boys should have things he couldn't have, and he determined to make up for it if he ever could.

From a relative he had inherited the farm near Hopalong, and had come there to live with his bride. Mrs. Manners thought her husband had great ability, if only she could help him to bring out the best that was within himself. It was her intention that they should develop the farm and enter into the life of the community, but her husband didn't want this kind of life. He was determined to build up a fortune in the quickest, easiest way, and as a result lost most of their funds through foolish speculations. Mrs. Manners had little sympathy for her husband's intense ambitions, but he was adamant, and there was nothing she could do to change him.

One of Mr. Manners' beliefs was that oil existed somewhere in the neighborhood. To test this theory he went east, made an intensive study of all the literature on the subject, and hired a geologist to help him with his maps. This geologist was Mr. Franton.

By the time the study was completed, both men had arrived at the conclusion that Sandy Hill might have oil. But at this point the men disagreed. Mr. Manners claimed that since he had hired Mr. Franton to work for him, all the discoveries they had made belonged to him. Mr. Franton, on the contrary, insisted he had worked on the Sandy Hill portion of the project on his free time, that Mr. Manners had never mentioned oil to him, and that he was the rightful owner.

This was a difficult legal matter to decide. Mr. Manners was certainly entitled to the work of his employee. But Mr. Franton had unquestionably worked on the Sandy Hill project independently. Mr. Manners claimed that Mr. Franton had relied on information supplied by him, and Mr. Franton denied it. This was the point in dispute.

It would have taken a long court battle to decide the matter, but neither man dared to go to court. They both realized that the big oil companies could easily beat them out for the leases they needed. Mr. Franton suggested that they compromise and form a partnership, but Mr. Manners refused. Not only did he want everything for himself, but he believed that Mr. Franton was trying to cheat him.

Mr. Franton, having run through a long streak of bad luck, decided to move west with his family, where he might study the Sandy Hill project on the spot. But the family's troubles were far from ended. On the way their daughter Marilyn contracted measles. This was a real predicament, for they were nearly penniless, and to stay at an expensive hotel until she was well would eat up their capital and leave them stranded. Marilyn's attack did not appear to be at all severe, and so they decided to go ahead anyway. Upon arriving at the farm they kept Marilyn hidden for several days. Mr. Franton was afraid of trouble with the health authorities for having brought a child with a contagious disease, and didn't intend to tell anyone about her until all signs of the measles had disappeared. That was the reason no one had known about Marilyn.

Mr. Manners, of course, had not liked Mr. Franton's move. But he pretended to be cordial, and invited the Frantons to stay at a second farm he had just bought cheaply. It was his intention to burn the family out. After the old house was destroyed, they would have been so destitute that Mr. Manners believed it would be much easier for him to reach a favorable settlement with them.

One morning he got his opportunity to set the house afire. Mr. Franton was away from home. Mrs. Franton walked out of the house toward the barn, presumably leaving the child asleep. But little Marilyn awakened, and toddled outside in quest of her mother. She lost sight of her speedily, and stumbled down a side path back of the hen house.

With the house now empty of people, Mr. Manners set off the fire he had prepared for, the flames spreading quickly and exploding the oil heater. At the sound of the explosion Mrs. Franton came out of the barn. Believing her baby to be asleep in the house, to the watching Mr. Manners' unspeakable horror, she ran into the flaming house in a futile rescue attempt. Mr. Franton returned just in time to see his wife dash into the flames. He knew that nothing except the baby could have led her to run into a burning house, and believed both his wife and daughter had perished.

Evidently overcome by grief, his mind and spirit seemed to break completely, and he wandered off toward the woods.

There was no one left to take care of Marilyn, so Mr. Manners was forced to take her home with him. Griefstricken, he confessed the whole story to his wife, who was fully as shocked as he was. Mr. Manners was seriously ill for a time, but he eventually recovered and they were very careful that the doctor should not see Marilyn when he visited.

After Mr. Manners recovered, they had to decide what to do with the little girl. Mrs. Manners would have liked to keep her, but of course that was impossible. An investigation might have disclosed Mr. Manners' close connection with the Frantons and their dispute. So they looked around for a suitable home.

Mr. Fontaine was a kindly, hard-working, and prosperous farmer, while his wife had frequently expressed a wish for a daughter. Surely a little girl would be welcome there, so early one morning Mr. Manners drove Marilyn down to the Fontaine farm and left her just inside the gateway.

Then Mr. Manners searched for Mr. Franton, and discovered him living as a hermit up in Rainbow Gulch, in an old cabin he had found. Mr. Franton seemed confused about his own identity and to have no memory of how he got there.

Mr. Manners did what he could to provide for the hermit. He brought him supplies, and then he arranged for the non-communicative José to carry food and clothes up to the gulch. Finally, not wanting to be seen in that neighborhood himself, he turned the whole job over to José. José did exactly what he was paid to do, and asked no questions.

But Mr. Manners did not give up his claims. The death of Mrs. Franton was an accident, and he had done his best to provide for Mr. Franton and Marilyn. He believed the oil discoveries were his, and he determined to claim them. If anything, he became more ruthless than ever.

It took time to clear up the matter of the leases, and the final step was an aerial survey of Sandy Hill to check the maps and make sure everything was in order. It was on this photographing mission that the plane crashed, and Mr. Manners was carried away to the gulch by the hermit. Mrs. Manners knew about the flight, but when only the body of the pilot was found in the plane, she supposed her husband must have stayed behind after all. Now she had learned the truth. She no longer wanted anything to do with the leases. It was evil money to her, and she felt that she still had a moral obligation to Marilyn for all the misfortunes they had caused her.

Her listeners could easily guess the rest of the story: how Mr. Manners had finally told the hermit that his daughter was still alive; how the hermit had hung about the Fontaine farm watching for Marilyn, until he had finally lured her away with him.

They were still thinking about this strange story when a nurse approached them.

"Are you Mr. Fontaine? I have a telephone call for you from Captain Leland of the forest rangers."

CHAPTER 16.

OVER THE RAINBOW

Just what target the parachutist was aiming for, the boys couldn't tell. From the air they must have spotted a clear space, and the man had jumped for it. The boys were unable to see just where the man landed, although it was on the far side of the gulch. They saw the jumper free himself from the parachute, and then both the man and his chute were lost to view.

"They wouldn't have dropped a man unless they had a good expectation of picking him up again," Ted observed. How could they pick him up? No plane except a helicopter could do that. A helicopter! Then that meant there really was a helicopter on the way, offering them a chance of rescue!

"A helicopter needs room for those big swinging blades." Bob was thinking out loud. "There isn't any clear spot on our side of the gulch, or the parachutist would have aimed for that. Instead he picked out a spot on the other side, a small patch that the fire must have swept past without touching, due to the twistings and turnings of the gulch. We've got to reach the parachutist, or he has to reach us."

How could they reach him? Back around the head of the gulch, the way they had come? No, the fire was still burning heavily in that direction. Then down the gulch and up again? No, there were few trails leading down the side of the gulch; besides, it was still burning below.

"There's only one way to do it—over the Rainbow!"

It took considerable nerve for Bob to lead them toward the Rainbow, toward the main line of the fire instead of away from it. But it must be all right, they must have been able to see from the air that there was a clear path to the Rainbow, and that was why they had decided to do it this way.

Bob's logic soon proved correct. By slowly following along the rim of the gulch they managed to reach the Rainbow without approaching too closely to the flames or heavy smoke. Overhead the airplane was still circling. Ted looked up at the Rainbow with misgivings. The center of the formation arched some fifty feet above their heads, and the climb looked treacherous with slippery footholds. Fortunately, this was the easier side. The other side would have been nearly impossible with Tony clinging to them.

At least their climb up the hill a little earlier had taught them one lesson. Their slippery shoes were going to be no help to them, and they took them off.

"Should I take my shoes off, too?" asked Tony.

"No, I guess you won't have to," Bob decided, for he knew that Tony couldn't make a climb like this. "I'll carry you the way the firemen do." He lifted her over his shoulder and told her how to hang on so she would impede him as little as possible.

"I'll go ahead and give you a hand," Ted offered

Before he could become too aware of the dangers he faced, Ted began the climb. He tested each rock with his hands before he grasped it firmly and trusted his weight to it. Several of them pulled loose, but he found a sufficient number of firm rocks to help him upward. Supporting his hands for the moment, they supported his feet a little later, as he slowly mounted the wall. He didn't look down into the yawning chasm below, but every couple of feet he stopped to give Bob an assist or to guide him onto the best footing. Tony was very still and almost immovable.

About halfway up Ted encountered difficulties. There were no holds just above, and he had to make his way sideways until he could reach a better spot. When he did, he began to inch upward slowly again, little by little, barely a foot at a time, carefully feeling for each rock. Bob followed the path he had chosen.

And then, as he reached out above, feeling for some support that would carry them up the last ten feet to the summit, his hand encountered smooth rock. There was nothing above to give support and no way to move down with the others below him. He was strung up, unable to move. He had a good grip for the moment, and there was no danger of falling, but how long could he stay there, and what about the others? With Tony on his back, Bob was a good deal less mobile than Ted.

"I'm letting a rope down to you," called a voice from above. "Loop it around your waists if you can."

The parachutist had made the climb up the other side of the Rainbow! The rope was already dangling at his side, and Ted made a firm hitch about his chest, then dropped the end on down to Bob.

"Come on ahead," the ranger ordered. "I've got the rope looped around a rock, and it can't slip."

"Roger!" Ted responded.

While Bob stood still, Ted was helped up over the final edge. Then he and the ranger helped the others up, until all four stood safely upon the comparatively level summit of the arch.

"I'm Captain Leland of the forest rangers," their rescuer explained with a grin.

"I'm Ted Wilford, and this is Bob Fontaine, and his sister Tony."

"My name's Marilyn," said Tony, a little doubtfully, "—I think."

"When's the helicopter coming?" asked Bob.

"Then you caught on all right." Captain Leland smiled. "We may have about half an hour to wait, but we're all right where we are. There's no fire directly below, and on my side the main line of fire has swept past. We won't get the smoke from your side unless there's a shift of wind."

"Then we won't have to climb down the other side of the Rainbow?" asked Bob.

"Oh, no, the helicopter will be able to pick us up from here. I have a portable transmitter to talk it in."

The airplane was still in the sky above them, and Tony asked, "When is it going to come down and take us home?"

"Oh, we're not going to ride in that plane, Marilyn. We're going to have a ride in a different kind of plane that doesn't have any wings."

Captain Leland was on the radio repeatedly, talking with the planes overhead, which in turn relayed information about the helicopter. Time moved slowly, and though the boys began to fear that perhaps the helicopter wasn't going to get there before the fire drew too close along the eastern edge of the gulch and the smoke became overpowering, the captain seemed very cheerful.

"Will there be any trouble with air currents over a fire?" asked Ted.

"Don't worry about that, Ted. We've got the best equipment in the world, and men who know how to use it."

Actually, they had been on top of the Rainbow for only twenty minutes when the helicopter finally hove into sight.

"If you've flown before, you won't notice too much difference in the air," Captain Leland explained, "except it's a little noisier. It's the going up and coming down that seems queer at first. When the plane gets just above us you'll feel the downdraft from the rotors, but don't let it worry you. It won't be strong enough to do any harm."

In comparison to airplanes, the helicopter seemed to move rather slowly, but it must have been covering a good deal of ground, for in just a minute or two it had churned its way overhead. Once certain that the helicopter had spotted them, the other plane left on some other mission. Slowly the helicopter settled down toward them, lower and lower, until it stopped only a foot or two above the crest of the Rainbow.

Captain Leland ordered Ted to climb in first, and it seemed pointless to argue the matter. Bob was about to pick Tony up, but the Captain took her in his arms.

"I'll take her. These ladders are a little tricky if you're not used to them. You can steady it for me."

Half a minute later the captain and Tony were safely beside Ted. Bob followed, the ladder was up and the door closed, and the plane was drawing away from the bridge.

As they flew along, it was exciting to identify familiar scenes. At first the whole line of fire came into view, then the unburned portion of the forest appeared, followed by the familiar ridge, then the Kirstead farm, and finally Bob's, which he pointed out to Captain Leland. Tony was completely lost, but enthralled just the same.

"I believe we'll try to take you directly home," said the Captain. "Where will it be best to land? All we need is a little stretch of level ground, with no chance of the wheels or blades snagging on something."

"There's a meadow behind our house," Bob pointed out. "That should be all right."

As Captain Leland consulted the pilot, Bob and Ted looked back toward the fire. It didn't look so big now, and it was hard to realize that those hungry flames had come very close to trapping them hopelessly.

The Captain returned to their side, and said, "That isn't very valuable timberland, and those acres of grass don't mean much. The rangers will probably record this as a small, unimportant fire. But it looks a lot bigger when you're down there in it."

He went on, "I've talked with the mobile ground station, and they know you're safe. It doesn't seem worthwhile to try to talk to your mother, since we'll be home almost before the call could get through. But they tell me your father has left to take a sick man to the hospital. Would you like to talk to him there?"

"Sure," said Bob eagerly.

"The connection's going through now. It should be ready in a moment."

When the call was through, Captain Leland spoke briefly, then put Bob on.

"Hello, Dad!" exclaimed Bob.

"Hello, Son," his father answered. "I can't believe it's you. Are you all right—and Tony and Ted?"

"Everything's swell, Dad, but you'd never guess where we are. We're about five hundred feet up in the air in a helicopter, and we're beginning to settle down over our farm."

"I'll see you soon, Bob."

As they touched the ground, they saw Mrs. Fontaine running toward them across the meadow. As she reached them she scooped Tony up and managed to get an arm about Bob. Then she hugged Ted, too. Her next thought was for her husband.

"We'll have to call him right away."

"I've talked to him from the plane, Mom. Who was the sick man he took to the hospital?"

"The hermit. He was badly burned by the time he got there."

"Oh." Then the hermit had been injured after all. "And Starlight?"

"She's all right, Bob. Had a hard ride and got sweated up, but there's not a burn on her. Give her a day's rest, and she'll be nearly over it. Meadowlark came home, too."

Captain Leland was introduced, and the boys themselves shook the Captain's hand warmly.

The crew also stepped out, but refused all thanks. The pilot said, "It's all in the day's work, buddy. You pay your taxes, and this is what you get."

The other man, who called himself "copilot and everything else," added, "I sometimes thought of getting a different job, like maybe in a jet, but there are days when I wouldn't trade this for anything."

Mrs. Fontaine invited them to stop at the house for lunch, but they declined. "We've got food on the plane, and we might be needed again soon. I would like a chance to freshen up a bit, though. It gets pretty hot and dirty sometimes."

"But not as hot as it could be," said the other man. "I'd rather fight fires from up there than down here. Listen for our radio, will you, Mac?"

Whether he meant one of the boys, or Captain Leland, they did not know, but if it was the Captain, he didn't seem to mind. The two young men ran across the field, and ducked their heads under the pump. They returned in a few minutes, and took off, waving their hands at the group.

The others walked slowly back toward the house. So much had happened that the boys had to be reminded to get some shoes on. Ted was asked to drive Captain Leland back to rejoin the rangers. Upon being reminded, Tony thanked the Captain with a kiss that left him smiling.

"If you wait for me," she told him, "I'll get my bank and give you all the money in it to pay for the ride."

"Why, Marilyn, I think you've already paid me far more than the ride was worth. I feel sure Uncle Sam will be ready to mark this 'settled in full.' "

At mention of the name "Marilyn," Mrs. Fontaine looked surprised, but she would not ask questions in front of the neighbors, who were still there.

When Ted returned, coffee and sandwiches were ready. Everyone was quiet, and Ted felt that they were marking time until Mr. Fontaine returned. Then they would find out about the hermit, and perhaps clear up the other mysteries.

"Tony" was trying to eat, though her eyes were drooping. Marilyn, Ted thought—if that was her name. But how had the hermit known? Marilyn, Marilyn. What did that remind him of? What had Cox told him about key words? A very vivid word which Mr. Franton would have no chance of forgetting. A word with letters scattered through the alphabet, but no repetitions. He spelled it out carefully. It met every test.

He jumped to his feet so suddenly that everyone looked at him in surprise. "Do you know where Mr. Cox is, Mrs. Fontaine? I've got something to tell him."

CHAPTER 17.

A SINGLE ACT OF VIOLENCE

Though Cox had been at the scene of the fire, apparently he left as soon as he had word about the rescue and returned to the farm. Ted went into a huddle with him.

"Do you remember that we almost broke that message using the key word, 'Maryland'? Well, how about 'Marilyn'?"

"Do you know something I don't, Ted? Maybe I *did* give up too easily."

Ted's copy of the message was unavailable, and he recalled having given his notebook to Nelson for some reason that morning. But Cox had a copy, and they set to work with it. The message began to come out: FIRST NAT . . .

"That'll do," said Cox suddenly. "First National Bank of some place or other. You can work the rest of it out for yourself, if you want to. Wasn't that Mr. Franton a cagey person after all? I figure he left the necessary papers in a bank safety-deposit drawer, so that even if I read the message I couldn't get at them."

"Can you get them now?"

"As long as he is living, I would need his consent. But I understand his condition is critical, and if he doesn't make it, it will require a court order."

"Yes, I just about had it figured out that the hermit was Mr. Franton. What do you expect to find in the drawer?"

"Proof that this little girl is his daughter, for one thing. And probably all the other valuable papers he possesses, even his claim to the oil leases, if he has such a right."

"Where are you going now?"

"I'm packing to leave. My work here is done. I'll want to talk with Mr. Fontaine before I go, and I'll see Mr. Franton, if they let me."

Mr. Fontaine and Nelson soon arrived home, and Ted went down to greet them.

Tony had been upstairs, but she came outside and was swept up into Mr. Fontaine's arms. Then, to everyone's surprise, she began to cry.

"Why, Tony, what's the matter?"

"It wasn't a game, was it? It was real."

Mr. Fontaine patted her gently. "Yes, Tony, I guess it was real. But it's all over now, and you did have a nice airplane ride, didn't you? I think you're very sleepy. I'm going to take you in the house."

Now Ted, Nelson, and Bob had a little time together, and were soon showing their relief by punching each other as if to show that they were all in one piece.

After Tony was asleep and the neighbors had left, they held a little conference—the Fontaines, Cox, Ted, and Nelson—in which everyone told everything he knew about the affair.

"Are we going to start calling Tony 'Marilyn,' Mom?" asked Bob.

"Why not? That seems to be her name, and she likes it."

"Yes," said Mr. Fontaine, "and I believe that Cox is right, the safety-deposit drawer will clear up the matter of the adoption in short order."

"Are we still going through with the adoption, Dad? It was one thing while she was homeless and without friends, but now that she may be rich, everything seems different."

"Why should things be different?" said Mr. Fontaine. "She loved us before, and she will love us still. I can't see that anything has changed. If it happens she should be wealthy, it will open a chance for a different kind of life for her as an adult, but while she is small we'll go on here just the way we always have."

"Is there any chance Mr. Franton will recover?" asked Ted.

"They didn't seem to think so at the hospital."

"Isn't it a shame that it had to happen to him just after he recovered his senses?" asked Mrs. Fontaine sympathetically.

Mr. Fontaine shook his head. "The doctor didn't seem to think that he had really recovered. It was just a remission, brought on by the shock of the fire. If he were to live, it wouldn't be as Mr. Franton, but as the hermit of Rainbow Gulch."

"Are we ever going to tell Tony about the hermit, Dad?"

"No, I think it would be better not to. She is entitled to know her real name, and something about her mother and her father. But she doesn't need to know the hermit was her father. As far as I am concerned, Mr. Franton died in that farmhouse fire two years ago."

"Yes, Dad," Bob agreed, "except that he came to life once more during those few hours when we needed him."

"I don't suppose Mr. Manners felt he was doing anything so terrible," Mrs. Fontaine mused. "He felt the rights to the oil were really his, and it was his own house he burned down. But out of his single act of violence everything else developed beyond his control."

"I feel grateful toward everyone," Bob went on, "especially when I think how many people it took today to save us: all the neighbors who discovered the fire in time, Nelson and his mirror, Mr. Franton who got well just in time, all the rangers, and Captain Leland and the helicopter crew. And Ted there—all the time just as cool as could be."

"Don't ever believe that!" Ted objected. "If I was calmer than you, it was only because I didn't have the decisions to make. I had a hunch you'd get us out all right."

"And we both knew we had to stay calm—for Marilyn."

Bob had one more thanks to give, and he took care of it later that night. When Ted and Nelson looked for him they found him standing with his head close to Starlight, speaking quietly in her ear.

"You great big wonderful girl. No other horse could have made it through that fire."

Ted signaled Nelson with a grin and they turned back to the house.

Printed in Great Britain
by Amazon